FIRM
COMMITMENT

Kate Denton

Harlequin Books

TORONTO • NEW YORK • LONDON
AMSTERDAM • PARIS • SYDNEY • HAMBURG
STOCKHOLM • ATHENS • TOKYO • MILAN

ISBN 0-373-03123-8

Harlequin Romance first edition May 1991

FIRM COMMITMENT

CHAPTER ONE

"JODY MARSHALL! Put me down this instant!" Anne's demand fell on deaf ears as Jody swung her in the air again and again. When he finally allowed her feet to return to solid ground, she swayed as he removed his arms from around her.

"You okay, Mom?"

"Yes . . . no thanks to you." She grasped his arm to steady herself until the vertigo passed.

"How will you ever get along without your favorite men, Mumsey?" James finished loading the back of his red Ford Bronco and came up behind his mother. He seized her by the waist, lifting her in imitation of his brother.

"James! Stop it! What's gotten into you and Jody?"

Laughing, he lowered her to the ground. "Poor little Mother. Getting too old and frail to handle youthful exuberance." He turned to his twin. "Guess it's a good thing we'll be out of her hair."

Anne Marshall nodded. "You're right about that. Thanks to you two, the hair is starting to turn gray. But just remember, I'm not too old or too little to do what needs to be done if you step out of line at college."

"Oooh!" They rolled their eyes in mock fear and Anne broke into giggles. Those two could always make her laugh—even on a day like this, when she was filled with misgivings and emptiness at the prospect of life without her eighteen-year-old sons.

The hot wind whipped Anne's skirt around her legs, and she had to brush her hair from her eyes as she looked at her twins. James and Jody were definitely David's sons. Tall and muscular, like him. Even in coloring they were his, their hair a chestnut brown, their eyes a deep chocolate. Anne was a petite five foot four; her coloring, with hair as golden as summer wheat and eyes of soft gray-blue, was a pale contrast to her sons'.

But Anne didn't mind the fact that they resembled her so little. Just the opposite. She'd always felt a sustained sense of pleasure that her sons were so much like David, as though it were a gift from fate, a way of helping her hold on to her memories of the only man she'd ever loved.

"We gotta go, you know?" Jody said. It was a question, almost a request for permission.

"I know." Anne nodded. *I will not cry,* she vowed silently. *I will not cry.*

Jody kissed one cheek, James the other. "Love you, Mom," they said in unison, their voices husky. They seemed close to tears themselves.

"Love you, too," Anne managed to answer in a steady voice. "Now off with you guys. I want you there before midnight."

Anne watched the cars—James's Bronco and Jody's blue Honda—until they disappeared around the corner, then she turned back toward the house, followed by Fred, the family's yellow Labrador retriever. "I will not cry," she said aloud, reaching down to pet Fred. The dog licked her hand, then tilted his head for a scratch behind the ears. "It's just us now, kid," she told the dog softly.

Anne opened the back door and entered the house through the kitchen, making a quick stop at the basket in the corner to pat a very pregnant Ginger, Fred's mate, before moving to the stove. She put a kettle on to boil; she'd drink some iced tea while she got dressed for dinner. It was Thursday. Thursday always meant dinner with Tyler.

A part of Anne wished she didn't have to go to Land's End, Tyler's home on Lake Travis, tonight. She wasn't up to it emotionally. This evening she was in a reflective mood. She wanted to do nothing more than curl up on the sofa with her glass of tea and think.

"Brood is more like it," she said, scolding herself as she pulled tea bags out of the canister on the cabinet. She dropped them into a pitcher, then filled it with boiling water. Frank—"Ole Blue Eyes"—a beige Siamese mix, rubbed against her legs, a clear message for his food bowl to be refilled. Anne obliged him, then fed the dogs before heading upstairs to her bedroom to change out of her denim sundress.

In spite of her reluctance to go out, Anne knew it would be good for her to be with Tyler. It was always good to be with Tyler. Especially tonight. He was the one person who would be able to empathize with her.

He'd miss the boys, too—almost as much as she would.

College... It seemed only a few short years ago that her sons were babies, and now they were young men. James had chosen Texas Christian University in Fort Worth, and Jody had picked Southern Methodist in Dallas. They didn't want to go to the same school, yet neither wanted to be far from the other. It had seemed the perfect solution.

Anne had secretly hoped the two would stay at home a little longer, attend the University of Texas in Austin, but they'd wanted to get away, to really experience college life. Even though she was reluctant to have the children leave, Anne knew it was time. She thought of the biblical quote "To everything there is a season, and a time to every purpose under the heaven." This was the time for letting go.

At five-thirty, Tyler's Cadillac Eldorado arrived. Every Thursday night since David had gone off to military duty overseas, Tyler had picked Anne up or sent a car so that she could come for dinner. At first, it had been the three of them in the formal dining room—Anne, Tyler, and Eva, Tyler's wife and David's mother. After the boys were born, sometimes they were included at the table. And sometimes, as they grew older, James and Jody preferred to sit in front of the TV in the den with their dinners on a tray, leaving the adults to their own conversation. Now both David and Eva were dead and the boys had gone—but still the tradition continued.

"WELL, YOU SEEM quite cheerful tonight. I was afraid it was going to be a rough evening." Tyler's smile, Anne knew, camouflaged the emptiness that echoed in his heart, as well as her own. He poured two glasses of wine and handed one to Anne, then gestured her outside toward one of the lounge chairs on the redwood deck. September evenings in central Texas were warm, often hot, and the breeze from the lake offered a cool respite.

"I promised you I wouldn't let this get me down," she said, "and I don't intend to. After all, it's a natural part of the mothering process. For eighteen years or so, you keep your children safe and secure. Then the time comes for them to spread their wings." She took a sip of the wine, a rich mellow Chablis.

"Wings for James and Jody—and for you too, Anne," Tyler said.

"It's funny. All the times I've felt overburdened by the single-parent responsibility—never having any time for myself, all those hours I spent helping them with homework, chauffeuring them around town, the endless laundry and ironing... But I guess if I'm really honest, I'll admit my identity's been tied up in that sort of thing, that existence."

"And now the butterfly emerges from the chrysalis." Tyler cocked his head to one side as he gave his daughter-in-law the once-over. "I like the new hairdo."

Anne smiled. Yesterday, she'd had her naturally curly shoulder-length hair trimmed to a bob and highlighted to cover the few emerging strands of gray she'd joked about with the boys. The curls now feath-

ered around her face. "I'm glad," she answered
truthfully. She respected Tyler. His opinion was important to her.

"The look takes years off—you could pass for a
young college student yourself."

"Please, Tyler. Now you're going too far. You
know full well I'm only a few months short of thirty-
seven. Hardly in the coed range."

"Thirty-seven!" Tyler said. "Sometimes I can't
believe it. Seems it was only yesterday your mother
called us to say you'd spent the afternoon in tears because 'your Davey' had moved."

Anne smiled. "Then you suggested Mother and I
come right out for a visit. And I ended up spending the
night."

"Yes, that was the first time. But not the last."

They laughed. It was an old joke. David and his
widowed mother, Eva, had been next-door neighbors
of Anne and her parents. Eva and Anne's mother,
Faith, were best friends. When Anne was born on
David's sixth birthday, he took her under his wing like
a little sister. Two only children, they were like very
special siblings for a half-dozen years. Then Eva married her boss, millionaire Tyler Cunningham, and she
and David moved from West Austin to Land's End.
Anne had missed her "big brother" terribly. Soon she
was a regular visitor at Tyler's lakefront home.

She remembered the exact moment David had
stopped considering her his kid sister. It was Christmas, during his last year at the naval academy, and he
was home for the holidays. There was a party. He had
playfully kissed her under the mistletoe, warning her

about all the wicked men in the world. Then the kiss had changed into something less brotherly.

For Anne it was a girlhood fantasy come true. She'd loved David ever since she could remember, had prayed nightly that he wouldn't find a special woman before she had a chance to grow up and enter the competition. Now, for the first time, David saw her as an adult, as a woman, and discovered he loved her, too.

He came home more often after that, even with his busy senior year at the academy and his flight training. Both their families had been hoping for just such an alliance; otherwise there likely would have been protests from all sides that Anne was too young. But there were none. David waited for her to graduate from high school, then they were married. Anne was only seventeen.

"You're far away," Tyler said.

"This house does that to me." She rose from her chair and walked over to the deck railing. "So many memories."

"But most of them good ones?"

"Yes," she said, "mostly good ones."

Tyler walked over to her and held out a hand. "Let's go in to dinner."

The meal was festive as usual. For years, Eva had suffered from multiple sclerosis, and as the disease progressed, she had stopped going out. As a result these family dinners had become an important part of her life, their lives. Though Eva was no longer with them, Tyler and Anne still regarded these occasions as special, so Anne tried to dress the part. Tonight she wore a blue-and-purple paisley shirtwaist dress of soft challis, and sling pumps. Tyler, as always, wore a jacket and tie. And, as always, there were fresh-cut flowers on the table.

This evening, Hannah, the cook and housekeeper, served grilled catfish, rice, a salad of fresh spinach and tiny cherry tomatoes, and a loaf of homemade bread with rosettes of butter. Tyler had carried the bottle of Chablis to the table and filled the wine glasses beside their plates.

He pulled out Anne's chair, then sat down himself. "So, are you all set for Monday?" he asked.

"I get weak-kneed every time I think about it. Do you really want me to do this? Are you sure Bennett Weston wants to take a novice into his firm? I feel like such a babe in the woods."

Tyler smiled indulgently as he reiterated his position. "Anne, you're going to be a first-rate architect. Ben's lucky to have you. Maybe you're getting a late start, but you graduated near the top of your class—and you bring maturity that a twenty-two-year-old graduate wouldn't."

"I'm just not certain Weston's group is the right one for me. He doesn't usually accept associates right out of school. Raiding the best and brightest from other firms is more his style, from what I read."

"Well, now he's getting one of the best and brightest *before* some other firm latches on to her." Tyler chuckled at his own words.

Anne wasn't soothed by his lighthearted effort at reassurance. "But a college diploma, a few part-time jobs and some community volunteer work is the sum total of my experience. I would feel better if he'd at least taken the time to interview me.''

"I've been doing business with Ben a long time. I'm sure he felt he could trust my judgment. Believe me, he thinks it's a great idea. A great idea." Tyler reached for his wineglass and took a big swallow.

He seemed a bit fidgety, Anne thought. Not like Tyler at all. In fact, she couldn't remember ever seeing her father-in-law uneasy before. "Were your fingers crossed when you told me that?"

"Of course not," he answered, then took another sip of wine. "You spent a long time at the university, getting that degree. You could have done it a lot sooner, but you weren't going to neglect those boys in the process. I was so proud when you finally graduated. Still, an academic credential means little without some practical experience. And Weston's the best."

"I know, I know," Anne said, "and I *am* grateful for your help. But I feel like a fraud even pretending I'm in the same league as the architects who work for him."

"You worry too much. It'll be fine, I promise. Remember, you're doing it as a favor to me."

The favor seemed to be the other way around, she thought. But in reality, Anne admitted that she'd accepted a position with Bennett Weston only at Tyler's insistence. She'd have been much happier starting her career at a less prestigious firm. But Tyler had always been so good to her—how could she thwart his wishes now? Even if her heart was in her throat every time she thought about going to work on Monday. He really wanted her to do this, so she'd agreed. She looked warily at Tyler, fingering her wineglass. "Does Mr. Weston know why you prevailed upon him to hire me?"

"You act like I coerced him," Tyler grumbled. "No, I kept our relationship out of it. Although I've wondered over the years whether you were ashamed of me. Never letting me use my influence on your behalf, always arguing about accepting any help from me…. I could have made things a whole lot easier for you, Anne."

She got up from her chair and moved to kiss him on the cheek, her hands resting on his shoulders. "You *did* make things easier. Just knowing you were there for us. And that you understood why I didn't want the boys to have an excess of material things growing up. You restrained all those grandfatherly urges to spoil them, and honored my wishes, instead."

Tyler patted her hands. "It wasn't easy, believe me. The temptation to indulge them was there all the time."

"Oh, I know," she said. "I really do. And I'd probably have felt the same way if I were you. But I've valued my independence—even when I complained about it. I wanted the boys to have a normal life, to understand what it was like to depend on income from a part-time job. I know one day they'll come into a lot of money from you. I just want them to appreciate it." She sat back down in her chair.

"You've done a wonderful job with my grandsons," Tyler said. He reached out for her hand and squeezed it as he stared into her eyes. "Ben Weston has no idea you're my daughter-in-law. You can just go to his office on Monday and start off like it's any other job.''

Working with an architect of Bennett Weston's reputation could hardly be described as ''any other job,'' Anne thought. Nevertheless, she smiled at Tyler.

He acknowledged her smile, recognizing it as acquiescence. ''Now let's forget business and enjoy Hannah's dinner,'' he said, his voice happily victorious. ''Try a piece of her new wheat bread.''

BENNETT WESTON'S architectural firm was located in a renovated house on San Antonio Street, one of several old residences he had restored. Anne paused on the front sidewalk and nervously smoothed the collar of her new navy suit and adjusted the bow of the navy-and-green print blouse. After years of sweats and jeans, she'd recently invested in several suits in order to achieve a corporate ''dress for success'' look. She wanted Ben Weston and the other members of his firm to understand her serious commitment to a career—even if she was making a late start.

Anne opened the gate of the white wrought-iron fence enclosing the lot and paused in the yard to read a historical marker. According to the marker, the structure had been home to a foreign legation, during the years of the Republic of Texas, before Texas had joined the United States. She climbed the steps to the front porch, noting the simple engraved brass plate that read: Bennett Weston and Associates, Inc., Member American Institute of Architects. The double front doors were curtained with gathered sheers and Anne hesitated as she reached for the knob. She took a deep breath. "Well, here goes nothing," she muttered to herself.

She entered a reception area where a gray-haired woman sat in front of a computer terminal, her eyes fixed on the screen. She looked up as Anne entered.

"Hello, I'm Anne Marshall."

"Yes, Ms. Marshall. I'm Billie Potter. Ben's expecting you." She got up from her chair and gestured toward an open door down the hall. "This way."

Ben, thought Anne. So, the atmosphere is informal around here. That would suit her fine. She was too used to school and homemaking and mothering to make a swift transition into a rigid business environment.

A man sitting behind an old-fashioned double-pedestal oak desk looked up as they entered his office. "This is Ms. Marshall," Billie said making introductions. She nodded at Anne. "Mr. Weston."

"Have a chair," he said curtly as he rose from his seat. "Billie—" he turned to the secretary "—do you think you can get these out this morning?" He handed her a sheaf of papers and sat down again.

The secretary nodded, then left the office, closing the door behind her.

For several moments Bennett Weston said nothing, silently reading Anne's résumé and occasionally glancing over at her as if he were forming a judgment. Anne was determined to measure up to his expectations. His perusal gave her time to do some examining herself. She'd seen pictures of Weston, had even glimpsed him from afar when he'd lectured at a campus forum. But that had been five or six years ago, and her back-row seat hadn't prepared her for the man in person.

His biography then had indicated he was in his mid-thirties. So now he was what? Fortyish? You couldn't tell, except for the smattering of gray strands woven through his dark hair. His eyes, expressionless, were as blue as the sky above Austin on a summer day, and his skin had a tanned outdoorsy look. She remembered reading that he liked water sports—sailing, waterskiing, fishing. But you wouldn't take him for a jock today. He was all business, dressed meticulously in a dark suit, expensive white shirt, tasteful striped tie, and handkerchief perfectly placed in his breast pocket.

Anne had always considered herself perceptive, good at sizing people up, but her initial impression of Bennett Weston proved inconclusive. Maybe because he hadn't given her much to go on. So far he hadn't asked her a single question, or even attempted small talk. He was scrutinizing her résumé as if seeing it for the first time. He raised his eyes to hers. He was handsome, even elegant, but at the same time he appeared remote, untouchable. He seemed too reserved, too stiff. If the eyes were the windows to the soul, she thought, then his were shuttered. He returned his attention to the résumé.

Was he married? She didn't know. But what difference did it make, anyway? Bennett Weston was going to be her boss, not a date. His marital status was irrelevant.

Even though Anne was single herself, she wanted no man in her life, *needed* no man in her life. She'd been officially widowed for almost five years—unofficially for much longer than that. The one man she'd loved was gone; there could be no substitute. And even if there could, the man before her probably wouldn't qualify.

"Where are you, Ms. Marshall?"

Anne's head jerked up. "What?"

"You seemed to be off in never-never land. I just asked you the time. My watch has stopped." He tapped the face of his watch.

Anne straightened in her chair. "I'm sorry. I guess my mind was drifting... It's nine-fifteen. Actually I was trying to recall when I heard you lecture," she hedged. "At the university. I know it was a few years ago."

"I've only lectured there twice. And the last time was probably half a dozen years ago." He leaned back in his chair, arms folded across his chest. "I was under the impression you'd just finished school."

"My education was primarily on a part-time basis," she said. "It took me longer than usual to finish. I thought Mr. Cunningham told you that."

He crossed one leg over the other and flicked a speck off his creased slacks. "Actually, Tyler—Mr. Cunningham—told me very little about you, Ms. Marshall." He returned his gaze to her.

From what she'd witnessed thus far, she imagined the man had *asked* very little about her. His attitude toward her was one of apathy, maybe even boredom. But she couldn't be certain. Reading him was like trying to read a book written in a foreign language. No, she decided, like reading a book with blank pages.

Anne leaned forward in her chair. "I may not have a lot of experience, but I can assure you I'll work hard and do a good job for you."

"I'm sure," he said, his tone flat, his expression still revealing nothing. Yet Anne thought she detected a trace of sarcasm in his voice. Did he resent her being pushed off on him? He got up abruptly and walked from his desk to the credenza, pouring himself a cup of coffee from a carafe. He did not offer her one. She wondered whether it had even occurred to him.

Ben Weston turned to face her. "Initially you'll be working with one of my associates, Mason Rogers. He's project captain for a small strip shopping center near Round Rock. He'll be in late next week and we'll talk about specific duties then." He drank some of his coffee, then set the cup down. "Billie will show you to your office. Everyone else is out today and tomorrow, so if you need anything, just ask her. In the meantime, I've got an appointment." He walked out and left her standing there. The meeting was over.

And just what was she supposed to do *this* week? she wondered. She'd certainly received no hint from him during this brief interview. His reactions surprised her, especially his cool indifference. Was it a mask covering his annoyance at being pressured to hire her? She'd been nervous about working for Bennett Weston, but had never expected such an aloof employer.

Oh, well, it was too soon to jump to conclusions. If Bennett Weston wasn't impressed with her now, he would be before long. She was willing to do whatever it took to become part of the team. She stood up and presumptuously poured herself a cup of coffee from Ben's carafe.

As she sipped, she took stock of her new employer's office. It was as unrevealing as the man himself. While professionally and expensively decorated in browns and black, his space held little warmth and no clue to the individual who spent his time there. There were no family photographs on the desk or matching credenza, no personal items or keepsakes. On second thought, Anne decided, perhaps it exactly resembled the man who spent his time there. Carrying her cup, she came out to ask Billie where she would be working.

For the next hour Anne sat—twiddling her thumbs and staring at the walls. The office assigned to her was practically bare, with only a desk, a drafting table, a swivel chair and one side chair. There were no pictures on the walls and no office supplies, except a pad of lined paper and a pencil in need of sharpening.

Still, the office was roomy and attractive, its one large window facing Wooldridge Park across the street. She could look out at the cars and people passing by and beyond that to the tree-shaded slopes of the park. In earlier days, Austinites used to sit on the carpetlike grass, watching performances in the old bandstand centered at the bottom of the incline. Anne liked the setting, a reminder of a simpler life and a simpler Austin. She felt comfortable here. As far as her office went, Bennett Weston had treated her well.

She leaned back in her chair and mentally decorated the space—a few paintings, a couple of plants, maybe even a small area rug. She'd have to control herself, though, and remember to keep it professional. No photographs of the boys or the Marshall menagerie on her desk. Just a few prints and some plants and the rug—that was all she'd add.

Anne rose from her chair and went out to the reception area. Billie was busily working on the material Ben had given her earlier that morning. "Excuse me," Anne said.

Billie went on typing. She was reading from a handwritten page, but earphones covered her ears, the wires running to a cassette player on the desk.

"Excuse me," Anne said again and tapped Billie on the shoulder.

The secretary looked up and lifted one earphone.

"I need some supplies."

Billie gestured to a cabinet against the wall and resumed typing.

The cabinet was full of all sorts of office materials. Anne took a stapler and box of staples, tablets, pens. There was even a brand-new, still-in-its-box calculator. Her arms laden, she returned to her office to get settled.

Anne was back at the supply cabinet looking for a calendar and some paper clips when Ben Weston returned. He nodded at Anne, then moved to Billie's desk and gestured at the wall clock. "Dammit, Billie," he growled, "why are you still here? You should have gone to lunch thirty minutes ago."

"But you needed these reports, and besides, I didn't want to leave the office unattended. I know you have another meeting at one. Oh, I almost forgot, Rosalind called." She handed Ben a pink message slip.

"Ms. Marshall is here. She won't mind answering the phone." He didn't wait for Anne to respond. "Now out with you." He reached down, punched off the cassette player and opened Billie's bottom drawer to retrieve her purse. Then he took her arm to pull her from her chair and handed her the purse. In record time Billie was hustled out. He looked at Anne. "I'll be in my office. No calls," he said as he closed the door.

BILLIE RETURNED within thirty minutes. "It's late," she said to Anne. "You'd better get something to eat." Anne gratefully surrendered Billie's chair, and the older woman quickly sat down and resumed her typing.

Anne walked down the street, bought a takeout sandwich and a can of grapefruit juice, and sat on a bench in the park while she ate. It was a pleasantly mild day—not as humid as usual—and there was a soft breeze. Every now and then leaves would flutter overhead in the trees. A pair of squirrels scampered around the grass grabbing acorns in their nervous little paws. Anne felt peaceful. Even though her entry into the business world had been somewhat anticlimactic, the hour outdoors was reviving her spirits.

Several thick file folders and a couple of architectural magazines were on her desk when she returned. Ben Weston must have put them there during her absence. On top of the folders was a terse note from him: "You may want to review these," it said.

Anne spent the afternoon reading the material. Some of it was general, but mostly there were articles or clippings about the various projects designed by the Weston group. Several articles and promotion pieces were about La Gaviota, a hotel on the Gulf coast Ben had designed for Tyler a few years earlier.

La Gaviota—the sea gull. Like its name, the structure was inspired by the state's Spanish heritage. Since its opening, the hotel had consistently been five-star and had established Bennett Weston as *the* architect in the southwest. Anne picked up one of the magazines; its cover pictured the lavish resort and was captioned: "An experience of the senses. The ultimate escape."

Anne agreed. She'd visited the hotel as Tyler's guest on the first anniversary of its opening. It was difficult to describe the effect. The sensuality was subtle; nothing obvious, no round beds or heart-shaped bathtubs, no mirrors on the ceiling. Yet it had made her long for David. It would have been a time for Taittinger's—their favorite champagne—a time for room service, a time for lovemaking. But David wasn't there. Even though Anne knew it was time to accept that he'd never be with her again, she had no desire to return to La Gaviota. The memory, the longing, of that single visit was still painful.

"Ms. Marshall. Anne." Billie tapped on the door frame to attract her attention. "Could you sit at my desk and get the phone for a few minutes? Ben's already left for a meeting, and I need to run down to the post office and put these in the mail.'' She waved several envelopes at Anne.

''Sure.'' Anne nodded, grateful for the crumb of conversation. She wasn't used to isolation, to total quiet. Maybe she'd also bring a radio for her office.

The phone rang the minute Billie was out the door. Anne wondered for a moment how to answer it. She picked up the receiver and said, ''Bennett Weston and Associates.''

''Billie, I need to talk to Mr. Weston right away. It's Rosalind.'' The caller had a sexy foreign accent.

''I'm sorry, but this isn't Billie and Mr. Weston's not in,'' Anne said.

''Then please find him and have him call,'' the throaty voice instructed. The phone clicked in Anne's ear.

She stared at the receiver. The caller hadn't given her time to explain that she didn't know how to find Ben Weston. Who *was* this Rosalind, anyway? Clearly someone who felt she could call his office and demand his attention. Anne remembered Billie had told Ben about an earlier call from the woman. Had he not responded quickly enough?

Billie soon returned from her errand. Anne stood up and passed on the message.

''Oh, dear,'' Billie said. She immediately picked up the phone and punched in a number. ''Mr. Weston, please.'' A couple of moments passed. ''Ben, a call just came in. Rosalind needs you.'' Billie hung up and, without a word to Anne, resumed her typing on the computer.

Anne stood fixed in place for a few moments, then headed back to her office. She sat at her desk, tapping a pencil. What was that all about? Was Rosalind Bennett Weston's wife? He didn't wear a wedding ring—but then not all married men did. Perhaps she was a girlfriend. Whatever, she had to be important to Ben, considering the way Billie jumped to transmit her messages.

What am I doing? Anne wondered. *Who cares anyway? Not me. Bennett Weston is my boss—nothing more, nothing less.* But it was the second time she'd told herself that today. Why did she have to keep reminding herself? Anne shook her head. "Don't be a twit," she grumbled aloud. Obviously she needed to concentrate on architecture and not on architects. What a fine mess she was making of this first day. She picked up the papers and went back to reading.

CHAPTER TWO

ANNE PULLED the station wagon into the driveway and sat there a moment staring at the house, a two-story combination of stone and clapboard siding painted a soft gray. Although it needed a fresh coat of paint, the house was a source of comfort to her—a real home. The only one she'd ever known. She'd grown up here. Then, soon after their marriage, she and David had bought it from her parents. Anne's father had been transferred to Arizona and the young couple couldn't bear to let strangers take the place over. The house was part of her, although lately it seemed too empty.

Well, at least someone's here to welcome me home, she thought, as she spotted Fred and Frank hurrying to the back gate to meet her. Poor old potbellied Ginger. She seldom trotted through the animal door to frolic with Fred now. Instead, she stayed in her basket, waiting for the puppies to arrive. Anne fretted about the likelihood of being away from home when they were born. Even though it was Ginger's second litter, Anne had acted as midwife for the first and wished she could participate this time, too.

That old mothering instinct continued to kick in. With the boys gone, she was shifting all her attention to the animals. But the pets would have to get through the days without her. She was now a career woman—and she could just imagine her strictly business boss giving her time off to attend a canine birthing.

She unlocked the back door and went in, setting her purse and briefcase on the kitchen counter. Sure enough, there was Ginger curled up in her doggie bed in the corner. Anne bent down and rubbed her back. "Hello, old girl. How are you feeling?" The gentle Lab wagged her tail in reply, slapping it noisily against the side of the basket.

Anne kicked off her high heels and dropped her suit jacket over a chair. After putting down fresh food and water for the animals, she poured herself a diet soda and went upstairs to change out of her work clothes. She paused on the landing and listened. The house was so quiet. A giant wave of loneliness washed over her. This solitary life was going to take some getting used to.

Dressed in a mint-green jumpsuit, she came back downstairs and hurried to the den to turn on the television set for a little background chatter. Anne smiled. She'd always complained that the boys made too much noise, and now she missed all that talking and bickering and confusion.

For a few moments Anne listened to the local newscaster, then went into the kitchen to begin dinner—dinner for one. She took a single lamb chop from the refrigerator and put it in the oven. While it cooked, she made a small salad. That would be enough—with no gang of bottomless-pit teenage boys around to eat her out of house and home.

Tilted back in her reclining chair, Anne watched the national news, read the newspaper, then ate her dinner in front of an *I Love Lucy* rerun. Afterward, she looked over the architectural journals she'd brought home and was in bed by nine. The end of her first day as a career woman.

She sighed as she lay in her darkened bedroom staring through the window at the sliver of moon. She'd been tempted to call the boys, but restrained herself. She wasn't going to be a "smother," as James and Jody referred to a couple of their friends' mothers. *I have to turn them loose,* she thought. But at the same time, she felt strange with her new existence. And a little sad.

Tuesday was almost a repeat of Monday. She arrived at the office the same time as Bennett Weston, her boss uttering a perfunctory "Good morning, Ms. Marshall," before heading into his office. He remained there the rest of the morning, most of the time with the door closed, and Billie stayed glued to her computer.

Once again Anne was left to her own devices. She made a trip to her car for a box of belongings and spent some time personalizing her office. She placed a small radio and an African violet on her desk, a Dhurrie rug on the floor, then hung a watercolor and a couple of prints she'd had at home on the walls. The office now looked more appealing, though maybe she'd pick up another plant or two over the weekend. Even the undemonstrative Mr. Weston would probably voice his approval. Yet Anne was beginning to wonder if her employer would have preferred her stuffed in a broom closet somewhere.

You're being unfair, she told herself, *to automatically assume he dislikes you.* He and Billie weren't deliberately ignoring her; they were just extremely busy. It was probably a bad week to train a newcomer. Still, his morning greeting replayed in her head. "Good morning, Ms. Marshall." Ben called Billie—old enough to be his mother—by her first name, while Anne who was his contemporary, was *Ms.* Marshall.

The title seemed to indicate formality rather than deference. And even if he intended deference, Anne didn't like that, either. It would only confirm what she already suspected—that she was here simply as a favor to Tyler. She'd been independent too long to accept a handout. She wanted Ben to give her an assignment, any assignment. Sitting around like this, spending the hours reading files and journals, left her bored and restless. The hours crawled by.

Anne hated having unscheduled days on her hands. It didn't happen often. Of necessity she'd kept busy with the boys, with charity, with schoolwork. Unless she was occupied, there was too much time to think. A hectic schedule was her way of surviving, her defense against pain. Memories of David intruded whenever there was space. She wondered wistfully what her life would be like if he were still alive. Very, very different . . . "Enough of that," she admonished herself.

Returning from a late lunch—she'd again been assigned backup phone duty for Billie—Anne encountered Ben in the narrow rear hallway. He pressed against the wall, allowing her a wide berth to pass. It was almost as though he wanted to avoid any contact with her. He mumbled a faint "Good afternoon," as unanimated as his greeting that morning, before walking briskly out the door.

Anne returned to her desk. She had no idea how to handle this situation. Her first intuition, that Bennett Weston resented having her there, was being reinforced. Why would Tyler thrust her into an arrangement like this? Why would he compel someone to take her out of friendship or professional obligation or whatever it was?

But what could she do about it now? It would look terrible on her résumé if she resigned after only a few days, especially from a firm like Weston's. Potential employers would assume she'd been asked to leave, that there was something wrong with her. So she was stuck. If she hoped for a career in architecture, she was going to have to tough it out here, at least for a while.

Anne picked up another journal from her desk; this one also featured an article about La Gaviota. She forced her mind to linger on the resort. It was difficult to imagine her employer as its creator. He seemed more like the kind of man who would design glass-and-steel towers—cold monoliths for banking and finance.

Could the passionless man she was working for possibly have envisioned La Gaviota? Apparently so—but people did change. Could something have happened to change Ben? "Interesting to speculate on, but none of your business," she reminded herself, then picked up another file folder.

Anne looked at her watch, expecting it to be perhaps four-thirty or quarter to five. But her watch said five-thirty. She'd become so engrossed in her reading that the time had slipped away. She looked out the window, at the dark clouds threatening a thunderstorm. She quickly straightened her desk and grabbed her jacket. The lights in the reception area were on, but Billie had already left. Ben, apparently, was still working. Anne went out the back exit to the parking area, then got into her car and turned the key. Nothing happened. She tried the engine again. The car wouldn't start. She heard the rumble of thunder and saw a flash of lightning in the southwest.

"Problems?" Ben Weston was calling through the car window. He must have come out behind her.

Anne rolled down the window. "It won't start."

"Let me give it a try," he said, opening the door.

Anne slid across the seat, wondering what made Ben think he'd have any more success at starting the car than she'd had.

When the engine failed to turn over, Ben pulled the hood release and got out to look at it. Anne followed, peering over his shoulder.

"Well, you've got a new battery," he said, "so that shouldn't be the problem. But I don't know what else it could be. I'm not very good at cars."

Glory be, thought Anne. The iron man was actually admitting a flaw. "I'd better go in and call a garage," she said.

About that time another burst of thunder resounded and big raindrops began to fall. "Forget the garage for now." Ben took her hand, pulling her toward his car. "You'll get soaked trying to do something about it. I'll take you home."

Anne didn't know what to say. Her hand tingled from Ben's grip, a reaction almost alien to her. "I don't want to trouble you," she argued.

Ben shrugged. "No problem. You can call a service truck from home and have them take care of it. Where do you live?"

Anne gave directions to her house in West Austin as Ben started his car. He was silent during the drive, except when confirming her instructions. "You said Loop One north?"

His assurance to the contrary, this side trip to her place would probably give him one more reason to be annoyed about having her around, Anne decided. As if he needed more.

He turned into her driveway and let her out by the front door. "Thanks," she said. "I really appreciate this."

"No problem," he repeated, and drove off into the rain.

WEDNESDAY BEGAN in a more promising fashion than the previous two days. Tyler had called the moment Anne arrived home the night before; when he'd learned about her car problem, he'd insisted on taking care of it, despite her protests. Her station wagon, now operable, was sitting in her driveway ready to take her to work.

The staff Billie introduced Anne to that morning were friendly, in contrast to their boss. She met three of the four associates—Ralph Best, Hank Gonzales, and Willie Pearson, who'd all been out attending an architectural conference. Mason Rogers, who Ben had said was in California, was the fourth associate member of the firm.

The group appeared closeknit, and she was pleased there seemed to be no resentment of her intrusion into their midst. She could hardly have blamed them if they did resent her. Here she was, the new kid on the block, hired right out of college and handed the second biggest office in the place. Only Ben's was larger. And hers was located on the first floor, right next to Ben's and Billie's, while the others' offices were upstairs.

Not only that, the former residence appeared to be in various stages of renovation. While the exterior and downstairs were near completion, the upstairs work apparently hadn't begun yet. Ralph and Hank each had a small office with fake mahogany paneling and linoleum-covered floors. Willie's space had the same dreary paneling and linoleum and, although it was larger, half was shared with Mason Rogers. There were a ladder and some paint cans in the storeroom, so obviously renovation was close at hand. For the time being, however, all the men were "roughing it." To Anne, the arrangement didn't seem quite fair.

She knew that each of the men had more experience than she did—*everyone* had more experience than she did. Didn't rank have its privileges at Weston and Associates?

But of course, she was the only employee who had Tyler Cunningham as a father-in-law. None of the men seemed aware of her connection to Tyler or of the fact that she wouldn't have this job without his intercession. Still, even if the men demonstrated no notice of it, Anne was beginning to realize that the repercussions of patronage, and yes, nepotism, went far beyond her original concerns.

Ben was in and out all that day. When he first arrived at nine-thirty, Anne was upstairs having a coffee break and getting acquainted with the guys. For her there was another cool "Good morning" from her boss. But for the men, there was a joke, which wasn't a joke, about standing around while there was work to be done. The preferential treatment embarrassed Anne; if the men were to be chastised, then she should be also.

Not that anyone had actually been doing anything wrong. She'd gone upstairs to give Ralph Best an express delivery and had stayed to share a cup of coffee. She'd only been there a couple of minutes when Ben came in. She had half a mind to tell him how unfair he was being—but what good would that do? Doubtless three grown men wouldn't appreciate a lone female coming to their defense. Especially one who was just starting a third day on the job. Neither would Ben. Anne had to remember she was on new turf; this wasn't home and she wasn't in charge here. She'd have to learn to hold her tongue and to squelch the maternal instincts.

The men quickly returned to work and Anne went back downstairs. Ben hadn't asked about her car. Obviously he didn't care. Obviously he'd rescued her the evening before only because, as her employer, he'd felt he had to come to her aid.

The rest of the morning she stayed in her office familiarizing herself with the computer, reading more architectural magazines, trying to keep busy.

Anne heard from Ben only once more that day, when he buzzed her on the intercom at twelve and asked her to answer the phone while Billie took lunch. She didn't mind occasionally filling in; there weren't many calls at noon, anyway. Yet she didn't like the idea of telephone duty as a regular chore. More troublesome, however, was the fact that Ben seemed to be avoiding all personal contact with her. The rest of the staff, picking up on Ben's "off limits" message, began following suit, and there was little interaction with any of them after that earlier coffee break.

Anne couldn't help feeling hurt. She'd worked temporary jobs in a few offices, and unofficial protocol called for at least a bit of protective interference on behalf of the new employee, such as ensuring that she had a partner at noontime. But not here. How could she possibly work in such an unsociable atmosphere? It went against her nature.

She sat at Billie's desk staring at the phone. Had Ben made his connection with Rosalind yesterday? It seemed that way, because there were no calls from her today. Only two clients, who left messages. Anne was relieved the woman hadn't called again while she was on phone duty. She couldn't quite understand why, but she felt a strange resentment toward the unknown Rosalind.

Was she jealous? Could it be she envied Ben, felt cheated because even someone as detached as he was had a personal relationship? But that was nonsense;

she didn't *want* anyone in her life. Still, Anne had to admit she'd been reminding herself of that fact more often the past few months—probably as a result of the boys' leaving.

Bennett Weston was out of the office the next day. When Anne asked whether he'd be in, Billie shook her head, responding that he was "spending some time with Rosalind."

Anne longed to ask Billie about Rosalind, but decided it would be presumptuous to do so. Maybe when she got to know Billie better she could.

With Ben out, the three men and Billie dropped their arms'-length attitudes and were more congenial. Billie herself asked if Anne would mind taking phone duty at twelve. Billie then left with Hank Gonzalez while Ralph and Willie waited for Anne. Anne doubted the men would have included her had their boss been present that day.

Despite the friendlier environment, Anne was again having second thoughts about whether she would fit in. She was used to being her own person and found it hard to adjust to the split demands of this workplace—one type of behavior when the boss was around and another when he was out. She began to wonder if she even wanted a job. She'd enjoyed college and had graduated near the top of her class, yet in truth, she'd pursued a degree in architecture simply because it had been David's career plan for himself. She liked being a full-time member of her neighborhood, felt satisfaction in contributing to the community with myriad volunteer activities. She'd been a homemaker so long—did she really want to change?

As she asked herself the question, she already knew the answer. What alternative did she have? Who would she be a homemaker for? Herself? The animals? "Wise up, lady," she muttered. "You have no choice." Volunteer activities, despite the great personal reward, brought no salary, and money was getting tight, what with two college-age boys. Naturally Tyler would race to the rescue if she needed anything, but Anne had fiercely protected her independence for years. She didn't want to start depending on Tyler as a financial buffer at this late date. She was going to get along here if it killed her.

Anne's schedule outside the office followed its predictable course, so on Thursday she dined with Tyler. As tired as she was from the new routine, her preference would have been to cancel, but she knew her father-in-law was eagerly awaiting all the details about her job.

Tyler plucked the cork from a bottle of champagne with a dramatic flourish. "I thought we'd toast your new career tonight." He filled two fluted glasses with the sparkling wine.

"Maybe your celebration is a little premature," Anne said wryly.

"Oh?" Tyler cocked an eyebrow and sat down on the arm of her chair. "Problems?"

"No, not exactly. I'm just not sure I'm cut out for the world of offices and office workers. And bosses."

Tyler studied her carefully. "Ben giving you a hard time?"

"Oh, no," she said. He *hadn't* given her any real problems, had in fact been almost deferential. How could she complain about that? It was his personality that troubled Anne. And the spillover effect it had on the others. "I just feel like a square peg in a round hole."

"Don't be so rough on yourself." Tyler's voice was sympathetic, yet chastising. "You'll be a round peg before you know it."

Anne smiled. "I wish I had your faith."

"You will. You will. Now drink up."

WHEN FRIDAY AFTERNOON came to an end, Anne felt drained. This first week of pretend work had been harder than she'd expected—probably more tiring than if she'd actually been given something meaningful to do. She picked up her purse and suit jacket and gratefully left the office for home. She needed the weekend to revitalize herself.

She bought a few things at the supermarket on the way home—milk, bread, dog food, coffee, bananas and a copy of *Good Housekeeping* magazine—shaking her head in amazement when she surveyed her solitary shopping bag and the grocery bill, which tallied less than a fourth of her normal expenditure. Life had changed in more ways than one with the boys in college.

MONDAY WAS MUCH THE SAME as the previous week. She'd asked Ben what she could do, and he'd told her to place a stack of tracings in the flat files. The project had kept her occupied for only a few hours. When she asked for something else, he suggested another menial task. Apparently all he was concerned with right now was keeping her out of his way.

Of course, he *was* busy. Everyone was busy—except Anne. Ben was always with a client, or on the telephone, or at his drafting table. Billie seemed to do the work of three secretaries. Ralph, Willie and Hank were either slaving away upstairs or out at one of the project sites. It just didn't make sense for her not to pitch in, too.

Ben hadn't said anything more about her working with Mason Rogers, maybe because Mason had been delayed in California. So why should Ben wait any longer to use her? In some meaningful way, that is. Whenever she managed to grab a few minutes of his time, to ask for something to do, he silenced her by assigning another run-of-the-mill duty. It was usually a task that fell within the purview of a student trainee, like running the blueprint machine or modifying details on the computer. Or it was a clerical job, like answering the phone or making a delivery.

Anything to appease her and get her out of the way, she decided. It didn't make sense to Anne that she'd been hired as an architect but was in fact functioning as a high-level drudge. What was she really? Where did she fit in?

She tried to corner Ben after lunch on Wednesday to talk about her concerns, but he brushed her aside. "I don't have time for this now," he said, heading out the door.

"Rosalind's waiting for him," Billie explained after Ben had left.

Of course. Rosalind. That name again. The woman called almost daily—sometimes more often—and how many hours did Ben spend away from the office because of her? This was the third time, Anne calculated, since she'd come to work there. Although his behavior had little to do with her, it was annoying. For one thing, it wasn't very professional. For another, he'd have more time to teach her the job if he weren't so busy with his private life.

She again thought about quizzing Billie. Or one of the men. But that just wouldn't do. Ben Weston might find out if she started asking questions, and Anne felt certain he wouldn't appreciate her prying into his affairs.

A second week of limited activity was topped by a totally unexpected amount in Anne's pay envelope on Friday. She knew then that she had to have some answers to her questions. She got to work early on Monday so that she could corner Ben the instant he arrived, talk to him before he got caught up in the nonstop bustle of the office.

Ben was standing at his desk, removing some file folders from a briefcase, when she entered his office. "What exactly are you paying me for?" She took the check from her purse and held it up for him to see.

"I'm afraid I don't understand the problem," he said.

"Then I'll explain." She spoke slowly, trying to keep the indignation she felt from showing in her voice. "I've spent two weeks in your firm, for the most part twiddling my thumbs while everyone else has too much to do. Then I get my first paycheck . . . a very generous paycheck, I might add. And I'm stunned. It's entirely too much for a starting salary, even if you *were* using me as an architect—which you aren't. I want to do the work I trained for, not be a junior-grade minion. And I want to be paid for what I do. I don't want a handout.'' She laid the check on his desk.

"Well, that's a new one. Someone complaining about being underworked and overpaid. Are you saying you don't need the money?''

"No, that's not what I'm saying. Not at all. But what I *need* has nothing to do with it. The point I'm trying to make is that my paycheck is entirely out of line with the work I've done since I joined the firm. It's probably the same salary you pay the other staff. That's not what I want.''

Ben eyed her curiously. "I see. So what are you suggesting I do?''

"First, pay me whatever you pay an architect who's just starting out. Then give me some real work to do.''

"Anything else?'' His face was expressionless, his blue eyes impenetrable. He moved away from her and took off his suit jacket to hang on the coat tree, then turned around, straightening his cuffs.

"Yes, one more thing. You need to get Billie some help. The workload around here is going to put the poor woman in her grave.''

For the first time Anne saw a flicker of real emotion in Ben's face. "You're right about Billie,'' he admitted. "I've been meaning to get someone else, but I haven't had time.''

"Then let *her* find someone. Or let me.''

"Do you have any other suggestions for revamping my office?" His distant undemonstrative look had returned.

"No, that's it. For the moment," she added.

"I'll consider what you've said." Ben sat down at his desk and picked up a file. She was dismissed. Again.

No one asked Anne to answer the phone during Monday's lunch hour. When she returned from her sandwich and stroll downtown, there was a note on her desk. It was short, yet polite. "Perhaps you could check the Sweets Catalogs and come up with ideas on whirlpools and spas for Cunningham's new hotel. I'd appreciate something by tomorrow. B. Weston."

Maybe the man wasn't as unapproachable as she'd thought. So he wasn't Mr. Personality. And so the assignment of going through the Sweets—a massive compilation of building products that was about twice the volume of the Encyclopedia Britannica—wouldn't tax her creativity. Still, he had listened to her.

She went to his office to thank him, but his door was closed. Apparently he'd gone out for lunch. She couldn't help noticing a phone message taped to his door: "Call Rosalind." There was that name again. Anne went back to her own office.

She picked up the note from Ben and reread it. Why had he waited until she was out to get back to her? He had certainly established a pattern with her, a pattern of ignoring or avoiding her whenever possible. But for what reason? That was puzzling. Ben Weston was turning out to be one of the most complicated men she'd ever met. Anne smiled, recalling that he was one of the few males over the age of twenty-one she'd had much contact with in a long time. She vowed to put Tyler through the third degree tomorrow evening. She wanted to learn more about her new employer.

BEN WAS SITTING at the reception desk using the computer and manning the phone when Anne arrived in the office on Thursday, a few minutes late since she'd waited for a cab. Instead of a suit, she wore a body-hugging red-knit dress today. She knew Tyler disliked the tailored look of suits, and there would be no time to change before her scheduled dinner with him. Ben glanced up as she entered. His eyes lingered a moment, then his customary closed expression returned.

The phone rang, drawing his attention. Even though Anne had gone into her office, the door was open and she couldn't help overhearing his conversation. It was clearly a female—and one he clearly didn't wish to talk to. "That's not possible," he said. "No, I'm really not fond of sushi. Thanks, Graciela, but my sailboat doesn't need any extra crew. If you'll excuse me, I'm late for a meeting."

He buzzed Anne on the intercom. "Would you mind getting the phone? Billie is out sick today and I'd prefer not to be disturbed."

"Unless it's Rosalind." Somehow the words just popped out. Anne hadn't meant to mention the woman.

"Unless it's Rosalind," Ben agreed.

Rosalind didn't call. Had he expected her to? Two other admirers did phone, and Anne took the messages to him later. Ben quickly eyed the call slips and tossed them in the wastebasket. There was apparently no room in his life for anyone but Rosalind. She was probably a spoiled society brat the way she made demands on his time, Anne decided. Probably a lot younger than Ben, but Anne had to admit the voice hadn't sounded that young—just sexy.

It started raining as Anne left the office building that afternoon. She stood on the porch to button her raincoat. Ben was right behind her and couldn't miss seeing Tyler's Cadillac parked in front of his Porsche on the street.

Red, Tyler's driver, got out with an umbrella and helped her into the car as Ben stood by his own car for a few moments, watching them with a frown on his face.

Why the disapproving look? Anne wondered, then smiled. For the first time it occurred to her that Ben might have misinterpreted her relationship with Tyler. The idea was laughable, but she could see how he might think she and Tyler had something going. After all, he didn't know Tyler was family.

Tyler was a handsome successful man, and it was quite possible for someone outside the family circle to put an entirely different face on his patronage. Ben had apparently chosen to do just that. Through the smoked-glass window, she could see him scowl. Well, at least there was a display of emotion. Anne was almost pleased. So he was a tiny bit human, after all. Was it possible he even smiled from time to time?

"WELL, HOW ARE YOU and Ben getting along?" Tyler asked.

"About like the Montagues and the Capulets. The Hatfields and McCoys. The Democrats and Republicans...."

"That well, hmm?" He seemed amused.

"Maybe I'm exaggerating—just a little," she said with a smile. Anne was seated across the dining table from Tyler, sipping a superb Bordeaux wine from his private cellar. "But then, you wouldn't say we're getting along like a house afire, either."

Tyler's expression changed. "Is there a problem? Do I need to talk to Ben?"

Anne grimaced. "You definitely don't need to talk to him. He's treating me well. I've got a lovely office, good pay.... It's just that..."

"What?" Tyler's voice now showed concern.

"Nothing really. But women's intuition tells me he doesn't want me there."

"You're using women's intuition on him?" Tyler shook his head. "The poor man—you females never play fair."

Anne leaned on her elbows and stared at Tyler. "Did he hire me under duress?"

"Is that more women's intuition?"

"Quit evading the question, Tyler. Did Ben Weston readily agree to give me a job, or did you have to use a little friendly persuasion? Come on, I'd like some answers. I want to know more about my employer."

"Now this is getting interesting." Tyler smiled knowingly. "Nice to see you curious about a handsome young man."

Anne sighed. "That's not what I mean and you know it." She took a forkful of her Caesar salad.

There were so many questions she needed to ask Tyler. Questions like "Who is Rosalind?" and "Why does he keep his emotions under wraps?" But she recognized that playful tone. Any more questions and her father-in-law would completely misinterpret her interest in Ben. She'd have to let the matter rest. For now, anyway.

CHAPTER THREE

"I HEARD THERE WAS a new addition to the office, but they didn't tell me she was so gorgeous." The architect was leaning against the doorjamb of Anne's office, a cup of coffee in one hand. "Mason Rogers," he said, coming in and extending the other.

"Anne Marshall." She rose from her chair to accept the handshake. "I've been looking forward to meeting you."

"Really? Well, the pleasure is all mine."

"I understand we'll be working together," Anne said. "When do you think we can talk about it?"

"I'd say right now, but I've got to finish a report on my trip. Ben's waiting for it. How about us getting better acquainted over lunch? We can discuss business then."

Anne readily agreed. Not that she was taken with Mason—he seemed a little too sure of himself for her taste. Still she'd been anticipating his return, wondering about the project Ben had mentioned on her first day. At least now she'd be getting involved. All the same, she hoped someone else would join them. Maybe one of the other guys. Or Billie.

But Mason had obviously envisioned an intimate lunch for two, and by the end of the meal Anne had decided he was the office Romeo. Mason was continually trying to touch her, pressing his hand against the small of her back as they walked to the table and frequently squeezing her arm. He even winked occasionally to ensure he wasn't being too subtle. No worry there. Mason Rogers was as subtle as a wrecking ball.

"Are you and Ben an item?"

Anne was startled. First, it seemed Ben thought she had something going with Tyler, and now it appeared Mason—and possibly the rest of the office—thought she'd been hired because of some personal interest of Ben's. The idea she'd been the object of such conjecture disturbed her. "No," she answered indignantly. "What makes you think that?"

"Well, you're the first woman to work for the firm. A couple of others have applied. We'd come to the conclusion there was an unwritten 'No females allowed' rule."

"You mean like the clubs little boys used to have? Surely Weston and Associates is a bit more sophisticated than that. Besides, there are supposed to be laws against such things." Concerned at sounding too strident, she smiled to soften the criticism.

Mason smiled back. "There ought to be laws against being as pretty as you are. You could certainly steal any man's heart away." He reached for her hand, but Anne adroitly slid it from the table onto her lap.

Unperturbed, Mason opened a package of soda crackers. "So you're not Ben Weston's love interest? Glad to hear it." He buttered his cracker. "Our boss is a fool, though, passing you up. But I guess it's in keeping with his image. As far as anyone can tell, there's been no female on the scene since his wife died. Not that he hasn't had plenty of chances. Women call the office all the time.'' Mason laughed. ''We could probably double our business if he'd be a little more accommodating with the ladies.''

''Maybe he's a one-woman man.'' Curious as she might be, Anne wasn't going to volunteer Rosalind's name. Let Mason do the gossiping. But he didn't seem to be aware of Rosalind's role in Ben's life.

''More like a no-woman man,'' he said, shrugging. ''He doesn't even act as though he likes women—except Billie, and she's more like his mother. I'm beginning to wonder what's wrong with the guy. Any red-blooded American male would be chasing you around the desk.''

Mason's comments annoyed her. ''I believe that's illegal. I think the term is 'sexual harassment.'''

''Oh, now, what's a little harassing between friends?'' Mason laughed again, and Anne gave him a weak smile in return.

He asked her to a movie that weekend, but she refused, telling him she didn't think coworkers should date. What she didn't tell Mason was that he wasn't her type. Tyler would probably accuse her of saying that about every man she met, but she still had no intention of going out with Mason Rogers. It had taken only a short lunch to decide that she disliked the man. And she'd already begun to worry about working with him. She would try to avoid causing a scene at the office, but she suspected it might take that to discourage him.

Ben was at Billie's desk when they returned. He hadn't asked Anne to answer the telephone again since their talk, but he wasn't above taking phone duty himself if Billie needed relief. He might be contemptuous of most women, but Ben was definitely solicitous of his secretary. *Maybe I should have become a secretary,* Anne thought ruefully. Clericals must be in real demand if Ben Weston found it necessary to cater to Billie's schedule. He certainly didn't appear this obliging to any of his other employees.

Ben looked up as they walked in, a scowl on his face. "I want to talk to you about that West Coast report," he grumbled to Mason.

He glanced at Anne and tossed two pink call slips across the desk. "Your messages." His tone surprised her. In the past he'd always been coldly polite; now he sounded almost disapproving.

Anne looked down at the slips of paper. One instructed her to call "the best looking man you know"—Jody's usual message. The other was more sedate—simply, "Call James." What was Ben so irritated about? Did he object to personal calls? She'd have to ask him, but there was no time to worry about that now. With a mother's concern, Anne hurried into her office to return the phone calls.

There was no crisis, just an invitation from the boys to fly up to Dallas-Fort Worth for the weekend and visit their campuses. Anne accepted eagerly. She wanted to see where they were living and meet their new friends.

THE WEEKEND WAS FUN and relaxing. Anne returned
to Austin feeling better than since the boys had left.
Both seemed to be enjoying college and doing well in
their studies. Life was progressing along a satisfying
course. She even felt rejuvenated enough to endure
another work week with Bennett Weston.

Monday at noon, he appeared in her office. "It's
lunchtime. Let's take a break."

Anne looked up. "Okay. I'll be going in a few minutes."

"No," he said. "I'm asking you to go with me."

Anne couldn't believe her eyes and ears. Standing
in front of her was Bennett Weston, the most aloof
uncommunicative person she'd ever met, asking her to
join him for lunch. She was tempted to comment on
his apparent change of heart, but said nothing, merely
nodding.

They walked out of the old house in silence, and she
waited for him to lead the way to his choice of a
neighborhood eating place. Instead he gestured toward his car, which was parked on the street again.
They drove to a seafood restaurant on Town Lake, a
place known for its exceptional food.

As they sat gazing at their menus, Anne became
more confused about his reasons for asking her to
lunch. It couldn't be he wanted her company. Although he observed the small courtesies, opening
doors and holding chairs, he seemed determined to
avoid touching her. Quite a contrast to Mason... His
conversation, too, was restrained, centering on the
weather and an article in the latest issue of *Architectural Digest*. Small talk was obviously the order of the

day. There were no flirtatious glances, no male-female games.

Anne had never doubted that, despite his obvious indifference to her, he found many women attractive. This assumption was laid to rest when a curvaceous redhead passed by their table and bumped his chair. The woman was beautiful, with pale, almost translucent skin, huge cinnamon-colored eyes and a lush figure set off by a clingy beige dress. Yet as she offered a coquettish apology, Ben hardly seemed to notice her. Anne wondered how he could resist such an open invitation—but he did.

Mason had said that Ben disliked women, and there had certainly been enough indications that he was right, but what about Rosalind? Anne wondered if the mysterious Rosalind could lift the veil of cold indifference from his eyes. Did the apathy vanish when Rosalind was around? Did his eyes smolder with desire when he looked at her? Was he simply a one-woman man? If so, surely it wouldn't hurt him to be civil to the rest of the female populace, would it?

The first course of their meal, a thick creamy crawfish bisque, was placed in front of them. Still Ben said little. For Anne, the silence was becoming uncomfortable.

"Has Billie been with you long?" It seemed a safe subject, since Ben was clearly fond of his secretary.

"I've known her all my life. She was my father's secretary until his death. I worry about her. Her health's not as good as it should be. She doesn't take care of herself—always skipping meals." Ben stopped, as though he had revealed more than he'd intended.

"But we're not here to discuss Billie." It didn't take any longer to find out what he did want to talk about. "I want you to leave Mason Rogers alone," he instructed. There was no mistaking the irritation in his voice or the coolness in his eyes.

"What are you talking about?"

"I'm talking about your tête-á-tête last week with one of my staff. How many men do you need in your life? First Tyler Cunningham, then those two gigolos who called, and now Mason. I won't have it."

"They aren't..." She started to set him straight about her sons but her sudden fury at his presumption forestalled the calm explanation she'd planned to give him. "Just how do you get the right to issue that kind of ultimatum?" she snapped, incensed by his unjust accusations.

"I'm the boss, that's how, and I hope I'm making myself clear," he said. "No hanky-panky in the office."

Anne felt the urge to laugh at the old-fashioned expression. But it would be bitter laughter and it would sound contemptuous. Why was Ben Weston determined to think the worst of her? "I'll try to keep my hands off Mason," she said sarcastically, thinking she'd have to try to keep Mason's hands off her. "But do you still plan to have us work together?"

"Looking forward to it, hmm?" Ben's thick dark eyebrows rose suggestively. "No, I no longer believe that's a good idea. Perhaps Ralph might be a better choice. He's married—happily, I might add. Do you understand what I've been saying?"

"Oh, I understand perfectly and I assure you that Ralph, Mason—*all* the males at Weston and Associates—are safe from what you consider my man-snaring ways."

"One would think Tyler Cunningham was a sufficient snare. It might not be a bad idea for you to cool it with him, too."

The man was impossible! So he *did* think there was a romantic relationship. She'd find it laughable, if she weren't so furious.

"Are you listening?" he asked.

"Oh, yes, I believe you're saying it's okay for the gander but not for the goose. Rosalind phones all the time, pulls you away from the office, leads you around with a ring in your nose—" Anne stopped. What on earth had possessed her to say such a thing? Especially to her boss.

But surprisingly he wasn't angry. "That she does," he admitted. Ben's expression had changed to one of amusement. His mouth curved in a soft smile.

Anne's annoyance faded under the warmth of that smile. The wintry look in his eyes thawed into a soothing sky-blue, and deep dimples appeared from nowhere. Ben Weston might not smile often, but when he did, he was devastating. Her heart suddenly seemed to be turning flip-flops.

But the change in his expression was only momentary and Ben's censuring look soon returned. "Now that we've got things straight, I suppose we can go." He signaled for the check.

"I agree," she said, glancing down at the plate of food she'd barely touched. "I seem to have lost my appetite."

THEY WERE SILENT on the way back to the office. When they arrived, Anne went inside while Ben parked the car. She entered her office to find an arrangement of fall blossoms—rust-colored mums, red oak leaves and yellow carnations—on her desk. Another indication that her sons were becoming men. The card said "Thanks for a great weekend" and was signed "J.J.," which was how they always signed joint gifts. An old private joke.

She was hanging her suit jacket on the coat tree when Ben walked into her office. He picked up the florist's card and read it aloud. "J.J.—another one?" He flipped the card back onto the desk. "How many men *are* there in your life, Ms. Marshall?"

"The flowers are from my sons. As for the number of men in my life, that's none of your business," Anne replied coldly.

He seemed not to hear about the boys, focusing instead on her retort. "It's my business when you appear to be carrying on a...an escort service in my office."

Anne's temper flared. "All right, Mr. Weston, if it'll make you happy, I'll see that there are no personal phone calls or flowers at the office from *any* of the men in my life, and I'll be absolutely angelic as far as your staff is—"

"That red dress you wore last week didn't look very angelic to me."

That did it. Anne was livid. How dared he make such ridiculous insinuations? He didn't *want* explanations; he'd already made up his mind about her. She could not possibly continue with this arrangement. "I quit," she said angrily.

"What?" Either Ben hadn't understood her or he was surprised that she'd finally stood up for herself.

"I said I quit. You're either ignoring me, or leaning on me and making nasty insinuations. It's obvious you've never wanted me here. Well, you win, Mr. Weston. I don't care to work in such a hostile situation." Just how far did he think he could go, anyway? She walked out of her office and headed to the rest room, leaving him standing there, a look of astonishment on his face.

Anne had returned to her desk and was packing the radio and the few other personal items she'd brought in when Billie entered her office. "Anne, don't go."

"I'm sorry. I don't stay where I'm not wanted."

"But you are," Billie said. "Ben wants you here."

"He has a funny way of showing it."

"Ben just told me himself."

"Then I suggest he tell *me* instead of sending you as his emissary," Anne snapped. She immediately felt contrite when she saw the stricken look on Billie's face. Yet what she'd said was exactly what she thought. Maybe she didn't have much practical work experience, but she did know that a successful working relationship required mutual respect.

She didn't have much respect for Bennett Weston and his ridiculous habit of jumping to conclusions. And obviously he didn't respect her, either, or such stupid notions would never have entered his mind. She couldn't stay in a no-win relationship. She just couldn't. What was she going to tell Tyler, though?

"Ben has a hard time apologizing," Billie said, her voice soft and quiet.

"Then it's about time he learned how," Anne retorted, her voice softer this time, too.

"You need to understand about Ben."

"I'm usually pretty understanding." Anne waited for Billie to say more.

"How can I explain? He's not always good with people," Billie began. "Ben grew up as something of a loner—a child of divorce, abandoned by his mother and left in the custody of a seemingly indifferent—yes, that describes him—an indifferent father. I worked for Everett Weston. He wasn't a bad man, but he couldn't bring himself to show any feeling, and he had absolutely no idea how to raise a child by himself. He shipped Ben off to an expensive military school, bought everything the boy wanted, but he never gave Ben what he really needed. A father's closeness. A feeling that his father loved him. I'm sure you'll understand how this affected Ben. But he *is* a good man. Just be patient with him. And please stay."

"I'm sorry he had an unhappy childhood, but that really has nothing to do with what's happened today."

Billie gave her a look of entreaty, a look the softhearted Anne couldn't resist.

"I'll stay the rest of the day," she finally said, uncertain exactly why she had agreed. "And maybe longer, if Mr. Weston asks me himself."

Billie's plump round face didn't look much happier, but she seemed to realize that this answer was the best she was going to get from Anne. She retreated quietly from the office.

Only minutes later, Ben buzzed Anne on the intercom and asked her to join him in his office. When she entered, he was holding the coffee carafe, but this time he passed a cup to Anne before pouring one for himself. He gestured for her to sit down.

"I'm sorry I intruded in your life," he said woodenly.

Anne didn't answer.

"It's just that Tyler's an associate of mine. I hate seeing him played for a fool."

"If this is your idea of an apology..." Anne set the coffee cup on the corner of his desk and started to rise.

"I'm botching it, hmm?" Ben's cupped hand stroked his chin. "You're quite right. Let me start over. I'm sorry. I promise I won't interfere in your life again."

For some reason, Anne believed him. She also believed that it almost choked him to say the words. "Apology accepted," she said.

"So you will stay?"

"Yes," she agreed, "for now."

"WHY DOES HE DISLIKE WOMEN?" Anne asked.

She and Tyler were seated at the dining table, enjoying one of Hannah's superb meals. Tonight it was mesquite-grilled chicken and corn soufflé.

"Maybe there's something to women's intuition, after all. So you picked that up?"

"It wasn't difficult. The only females he appears to tolerate are his secretary and Rosalind."

"You've met Rosalind?"

"No, I'm afraid I haven't had the honor, but the man is apparently crazy about her. A phone call and he jumps up like he's been poked with a cattle prod."

"What's so unusual about that?"

Anne sighed loudly. "She's too spoiled and demanding of his time."

"Well, she is quite young."

"That's no excuse."

Tyler frowned. "That's not like you, Anne."

She replayed Tyler's words in her mind as she got ready for bed that night. He was right. It wasn't like her to complain about another woman, especially one she'd never met. She sounded like a jealous schoolgirl.

But she'd guessed correctly: Rosalind was young. Tyler had confirmed that. Anne studied herself in the mirror. There were no two ways about it—what she was viewing was a near forty-year-old body. She pinched her midriff, managing to gather only a tiny bit of flesh, but the trimness gave her no comfort. She was a mature woman; the years of girlhood had slipped away almost without her realizing it. She was sure Rosalind didn't worry about her midriff or need to touch up her hair to cover the gray. She was probably still in her twenties.... Anne paused. Just why was she comparing herself with Rosalind? Why did it matter, anyway?

Still, the notion of Ben's romance was intriguing, and she couldn't cast it from her thoughts. How could a man so distant, so impersonal, maintain a torrid romance with a young demanding woman?

Anne tried to imagine them together—caressing, even making love. She envisioned Rosalind as dark-haired and sultry, with pouty lips and come-hither eyes. But when she tried to put Ben into the scene, it wouldn't work—he was still in a suit, still bandbox perfect. Would he risk ruining a crease in his slacks or mussing his neatly trimmed hair for a love tryst?

The image wouldn't crystallize. In fact, the more Anne thought about it, the more ludicrous it became.

ANNE FINALLY MET Rosalind. It was a Tuesday and Ben was in Houston. She'd had a busy morning, making title blocks on a stack of drawings and inserting print notes and captions with the Kroy machine. She hadn't even taken time for a cup of coffee.

Then, as if she didn't already have enough to do, Mason Rogers came by angling for another lunch date. Anne had already decided her first impression of Mason was correct; his main goal in life was to maneuver women into a quick romp in the hay.

Maybe that was all right for some women, but not for Anne. She had no interest in one-night stands. Besides, it had been so long since she'd made love she wasn't sure she'd still know what to do. But she definitely didn't intend to find out with someone like Mason. So she stayed in at lunch, handling phone duty again to avoid him.

Billie was away sick. Anne was beginning to worry about her; not only did the woman seem to have less energy every day, her breathing occasionally sounded forced.

Billie was an efficient old war-horse, but her daily routine would have taxed a whole herd of war-horses, and she simply couldn't keep it up. Her work appeared to be suffering. Anne began to wonder if she herself had been hired more as a backup for Billie than anything else.

Not that Ben had asked whether she could type—but he *had* asked if she was familiar with computers. A roundabout way of getting the same information. Anne was becoming increasingly sensitive about the work issue. Even though Ben was giving her more to do, most of the tasks she'd been assigned were glorified clerical duties. There had been nothing challenging, nothing she needed a degree to perform. A year of on-the-job training in an architectural office would have been sufficient.

She didn't mind helping out now and then. That was only fair. All the others, including Ben, supported Billie by getting the phone or running errands. But what was really needed was another secretary. She'd told Ben that and he had yet to take any action.

Anne was ready to do something about it herself—she'd fight Ben Weston later. Whatever his intentions might have been concerning her employment, she hadn't accepted this job to become an overpaid office flunky. Ben had never reduced her salary, so she'd just have to assume he was paying her for initiative. Before she could change her mind, she called an employment agency and requested that a person with secretarial experience be sent over for an interview.

Then she hung up and started to worry. Had she done the right thing? Maybe she should call back and cancel—

The telephone rang, interrupting her private debate. "Can you locate Mr. Weston for me?" Although Anne had heard the husky voice only once before, it was imprinted on her brain. She knew she was talking to Rosalind.

"I'm sorry," Anne said, "he's out of the city. I don't expect him back in the office today."

The voice became agitated, the foreign accent more pronounced. "I *know* he's gone to Houston, but can you find him? It's urgent."

Rosalind probably felt it was urgent every time she called. Yet from Anne's experience, Ben seemed to agree and always went running off like a trained hound. Far be it from Anne to interfere with his self-assigned role of fetching and retrieving. She picked up Billie's calendar and checked Ben's schedule. "According to his secretary's notes," Anne said, "he's out on some site inspections right now. I doubt we could catch him before he heads to the airport for the flight home. But he should be back in the office by the end of the day."

"That's too late," Rosalind moaned. "Is Billie there?"

"I'm sorry, she's ill today."

"Then you've got to help."

Help? How? Anne wondered. But, after all, Rosalind *was* important to Ben. "I can try," she said.

"Wonderful." Rosalind sounded relieved. "We'll be there soon." She hung up, leaving Anne gaping at the receiver, curious about what she needed and who the *we* might be. Thirty minutes later she had her answer.

Rosalind wasn't at all what Anne had expected. Not brunette, not sultry. Instead she was a young cherub with white-blond hair fastened with pink ribbons into puppy-dog ears. She was dressed in flowered overalls, a ruffled pink blouse, and pink sneakers. One tiny arm hugged a well-worn Winnie-the-Pooh. Anne guessed she was three, or maybe a petite four. The sexy voice that had filtered into Anne's thoughts belonged to Gretchen Schneider, Rosalind's nanny. The voice belied the woman's grandmotherly appearance.

"I'm sorry to burst in on you like this, but my baby sister in Cologne—Cologne, Germany—had an accident." She fumbled in her bag for a tissue. "Her condition is serious. Not only that—" she dabbed at her eyes "—she has four children who desperately need looking after. There's a flight leaving at four, but I need someone to watch Rosalind."

"Then I'm the one you're looking for." Anne stood up and wrapped an arm around Mrs. Schneider. "Just go on and take care of your sister and her family, and I'll take care of Rosalind."

Mrs. Schneider let out a grateful sigh and squeezed Anne in a quick hug. "Thank you so much. Please tell Mr. Weston how sorry I am. Tell him I'll be in touch. I know I'm leaving him in the lurch—especially since he missed so much work recently with Rosalind having chicken pox. Now this..."

"Don't worry," Anne answered, "we'll manage. I have lots of experience looking after children—I've got two sons of my own. Rosalind and I will get along just fine until Mr. Weston returns. And if he wants to, he can even bring his daughter to work with him. We'll figure something out."

Anne finally managed to get the nanny off to the airport in a taxi, and she and Rosalind stood eyeing each other. Anne wondered why she felt so pleased to discover Rosalind wasn't Ben's lover, but his daughter. The imagined romantic trysts were actually a father taking care of a little girl with chicken pox. These thoughts—which were interrupted by the men returning from lunch—generated an entirely new image of Ben Weston.

"Well, look who's here... Hello, Rosie," said Willie. "How's my favorite girl?"

Rosie broke into an enchanting giggle. "You're a flirt," she said to Willie.

"Only with beautiful girls," the tall black man replied, playfully patting the child's cheek.

Rosie giggled again.

"So you met Anne?" Willie asked.

Rosalind ducked her head, but her eyes, framed by the longest eyelashes Anne had ever seen, were huge with expectation.

"She sure did," Anne answered for her, then turned to Rosie. "I was just about to go out for lunch. Would you like to join me?"

The little girl smiled and nodded. Anne retrieved her purse from the desk, then helped Rosie retie the laces on her tennis shoes. Anne planned her usual takeout lunch—a sandwich and juice in the park. Rosie would enjoy watching the birds and the squirrels.

AT FIVE O'CLOCK Ben still hadn't returned. Anne wasn't sure what to do. It made no sense to stay at the office waiting for him. Besides, the little girl was getting restless, having been cooped up since their return from lunch. She'd finished a couple of drawings in a coloring book, napped on the couch in her father's office and then listened attentively as Anne read two storybooks Mrs. Schneider had left in a little tote bag.

Anne called Ben's home. There was no answer, so she left a message on the recording machine. To Rosalind she said, "Your daddy must be running late. Why don't you come home with me and he can pick you up there?"

Rosalind made no argument.

"I WISH I HAD A DOG." Rosalind was sitting on the floor next to Ginger's basket, stroking the dog's golden fur. "Miz Schneider's 'lergic."

"But you have Pooh Bear," Anne soothed. She walked over from the sink and placed a filled water dish on the floor. "And now that you've met Fred and Ginger, you can come visit them anytime you want."

"And Frank, too?"

"Frank, too." Anne smiled. Rosalind was a delightful child—bright, inquisitive, sweet and gentle. The kind of little girl Anne would have liked, if David... *Not the time to think about that,* Anne admonished herself.

"Are you a mommy?"

"Yes," Anne answered. "I have two boys. They're away at college."

"They're big then? Like Daddy?"

"Yes, big like Daddy." *Actually bigger,* Anne thought, estimating that Ben must be a couple of inches shorter than her six-foot-two inch sons.

"Do you get lonesome without them?"

"Sometimes," Anne admitted.

"I get lonesome for a mommy sometimes." Rosalind popped her thumb into her mouth. She looked sad, and maybe a little guilty, as though she'd given away a secret.

Rosalind watched expectantly, and when Anne didn't respond, she spoke again. "My mommy died."

"I'm sorry," Anne said. "Do you remember her?"

"No, I was just a little bitty baby. But Daddy says I look like her."

Anne could guess that she did. The child had few of Ben's features, only the pale blue eyes. Fortunately Rosalind's were much softer and more accepting than those of her father.

"I'd like to have another mommy." Again Rosalind ducked her head and again Anne could see the guilty look, the look that revealed the child felt she'd said too much.

"Maybe you will someday."

Rosalind shook her head. "Daddy says we can't always have everything we want."

What a cruel thing to tell a child. True, but cruel. Anne would have expected Ben Weston to be more sensitive when it came to his own child. From what she'd seen of him, however, she wasn't totally surprised. Sensitivity didn't seem to be one of his strengths.

Rosalind looked too pensive for one so young, as she returned her thumb to her mouth and wrapped her arm around Ginger. Anne's heart went out to the child.

"You know what I'm in the mood for?" Anne said.

"What?"

"Chocolate-chip cookies. How about you?"

"Yum!" Rosie jumped up from the floor and hurried over to Anne. Together they went to the pantry. "Uh-oh." Anne feigned surprise. "No cookies. I guess we'll just have to bake our own. Will you help me? Then we'll make spaghetti for supper."

"Chocolate-chip cookies and 'ghetti are my favorites," the little girl said gleefully.

"Mine, too. Now let me run upstairs and change clothes, then we can get started. Will you take care of Ginger while I'm gone?"

In answer, Rosie went back to the dog's basket and began stroking Ginger's head.

CHAPTER FOUR

THE SPAGHETTI SAUCE was simmering in a large cast-iron pan, and Rosalind was nibbling a sample from the first batch of cookies, when Ben's silver Porsche pulled up in the drive. Anne and Rosie could see the car from the kitchen window.

"Daddy's here," Rosie squealed, jumping off the chair she'd been standing on and running to open the back door. "Daddy, Daddy, we're making cookies." The youngster raced outside and met Ben just as he reached the kitchen steps. He picked her up and lifted her above his head, flour from the apron Anne had wrapped around Rosie dusting the jacket of his dark suit.

Ben didn't seem to mind the flour, and his rarely seen smile emerged while he listened to his daughter recount the day's adventures.

Anne wiped her hands with a dish towel and waited at the screen door for them to come in.

"You two ladies look very domestic," Ben said, a flicker of amusement in his eyes as he took in the aprons both Anne and Rosalind wore. He looked around tentatively. "Are you cooking something?"

"I didn't know how long you'd be—we were making dinner." Why did she suddenly feel so self-conscious?

"It was very kind of you to help out today." His voice had resumed the stiff reserved tone he always used with her.

"I've enjoyed it," Anne answered frankly.

"Well, I'll take this little monster off your hands now." He playfully tugged one of Rosie's puppy-dog tails as he spoke.

"But Daddy—" Rosalind's voice was pleading "—we can't leave. We've still got lots of cookies to bake and Anne's cooking 'ghetti."

"We've imposed on Ms. Marshall too much already, Rosalind." His serious tone seemed to suggest that he disliked being in Anne's debt.

"It's been no imposition," Anne said. "And how will I finish baking the cookies without Rosalind's help? Please stay. I'd enjoy the company."

"Your sons are out?"

"They're away at college."

His eyebrows lifted, but before he could say anything Rosalind interrupted. "Anne has two big boys. Big as you, Daddy. She's all lonely without them. We can stay, can't we?"

Ben looked at Rosalind. Clearly he wanted to leave, but the entreaty on the little girl's face would melt the hardest heart—even Bennett Weston's. "If you're sure we're not putting you out. You don't have anything else planned for the evening? A date?"

Anne ignored his question. "Why don't you make yourself comfortable." She gestured to a large blue recliner in a corner of the big country kitchen. "I'm sure I can rustle up a drink. What would you like? Wine, beer, scotch?"

"Maybe all three—it's been a rough day." He smiled at her, a begrudging smile, but it was very appealing nonetheless. Anne's stomach did a funny little flutter.

"How about scotch?" Ben said. "If you'll just point me in the right direction, I'll fix it."

Anne indicated the pantry with a motion of her hand. "Third shelf. Glasses in the cupboard over the dishwasher. Ice and seltzer, if you need it, in the refrigerator."

Anne, aided by Rosalind, spooned large dollops of dough onto a second cookie sheet, then slid it into the oven. She pulled a head of lettuce from the refrigerator to start a salad. Rosie returned to her favorite place at Ginger's side, while Ben settled in the easy chair with his drink and the newspaper. His suit jacket was draped over a kitchen chair and he'd loosened his tie and rolled up the sleeves of his white shirt. He looked less intimidating and more approachable than she'd ever seen him.

As she washed and drained the lettuce, Anne glanced over at her dinner guests. The scene was cozy and domestic, each of them busy with separate pursuits. Anne could read Rosie's thoughts; the little girl was trying to figure out how to talk Ben into getting a pet. Ben seemed to be buried in the newspaper, yet every now and then, Anne thought she could feel his eyes on her. Once, she turned and caught him quickly averting his gaze to Rosie and the dog.

For Anne, the evening was oddly comfortable, but also tense. She wasn't used to having another adult—especially a man—in the kitchen, sneaking glances at her while she cooked. It was unsettling, even though the meal was simple to prepare and demanded little concentration.

She couldn't help wondering what Ben Weston thought of her kitchen uniform of pink plaid jumpsuit and a chef's apron. Did he like this domestic Anne any better than the career woman? Or did he give any thought to her at all? He didn't attempt conversation, except to answer one of Rosalind's myriad questions every now and then. Anne heard him choke slightly on his drink when Rosie declared, "This is just like a real family!"

They ate around the old wooden table in the breakfast nook. "Like a family," Rosalind said again. Though his face didn't show it, Ben was probably perturbed.

"Eat your dinner, Rosalind," he instructed. The little girl obligingly ate two helpings of spaghetti, but Ben had to coax her to try a few bites of salad. He ate heartily, obviously enjoying the meal. Their conversation remained superficial and chatty, centering mostly on Rosalind. Judging by his behavior over dinner, Anne decided that Ben had little interest in her.

"This is a big house," he said casually. "Have you lived here long?"

"Since I was a child," she answered.

That was as far as he probed; apparently he didn't intend to personalize their relationship.

"I'll help you clean up," he said in his formal office voice, carrying his plate and Rosie's to the sink.

"No need for that," Anne told him. "I think someone's getting very tired."

Ben nodded as he observed Rosie's mouth stretched in a wide yawn. "Okay, we'll leave the dishes, but you can come in late tomorrow."

His suggestion annoyed Anne. He was treating her as if she were still on company time. She was surprised he hadn't reached for his wallet and offered to pay for the meal. "Don't concern yourself. I can make it by nine," she replied evenly.

"I...well then, Rosalind and I will say good-night. Thank you for...for everything. Say 'thank you,' Rosalind."

"Thank you." The little girl got down from her chair and said her goodbyes—giving Fred and Ginger a kiss and lifting Frank off the couch for a hug, then returning to wrap her arms around Anne. "I love you," she whispered as Anne hugged her back. Rosalind waved a final goodbye and exited through the screen door with Ben. She was clutching her Pooh Bear in one hand, and in the other, a sack of cookies Anne had insisted she take home.

Anne closed the door and latched it, watching while Ben fastened the seat belt around his daughter, then moved to the driver's side of the car. The engine started smoothly and the two roared off into the night. Only then did she begin clearing the table.

The time spent with the Westons tonight had brought up a number of questions. Rosalind had said her mother was dead. Why hadn't Tyler told her Ben was a widower? Was her father-in-law slyly playing matchmaker? It wouldn't be the first time. Tyler was a romantic at heart, trying to pair off the world. He hadn't succeeded with Anne. Despite repeated attempts, he'd never managed to bring a man into her life for more than a few hours.

Anne rinsed the plates and arranged them in the dishwasher, then poured the leftover spaghetti sauce into a plastic container. Thinking he could pair her off with Ben Weston was Tyler's most ridiculous effort yet. Ben was a walking, talking automaton with a blue-eyed stare that could cause frostbite in August.

Besides, he appeared to be a misanthrope. Or a misogynist, anyway. Certainly, his less-than-civil treatment of her and the way he brushed off other women seemed to indicate that. Anne had thought his attitude was the result of his infatuation with Rosalind—that other Rosalind, the one she'd conjured up from a voice on the phone. But apparently Mason Rogers was right about Ben Weston's "no females allowed" rule, both personally and professionally.

If she hadn't been away from the dating scene so long, Anne might have recognized the signals sooner. Even Mason, who couldn't read *her*, had noticed them. The fact was that Ben didn't particularly like women, and there didn't seem to be any room for one in his life. His life was like the car he drove, she thought wryly, a two-seater with space only for him and his daughter.

Yet there was an indefinable something about Bennett Weston that tugged at Anne's emotions; perhaps she'd sensed a hidden sadness within him. Observing him, first at work and then this evening with his daughter, she thought she was beginning to understand Ben a bit more.

Obviously he was still hurting from the loss of his wife. But mourning couldn't go on forever. No one knew that better than Anne. And if she ever got the chance, she would tell Ben Weston it was time to stop grieving and start living again.

WHEN BEN WALKED into her office the next morning, the last thing Anne expected was an argument.

"I just wanted to say thanks for the dinner," he began.

"You're welcome. I loved having you and Rosie."

"Well, you saved my life—filling in and all. I'm sure Mrs. Schneider is grateful, too. So thanks again." He glanced around her office, as though searching for an excuse to stay longer. Apparently he found none since he turned and started to leave.

"By the way..." Anne called.

He stopped and turned back to her.

"Where is Rosie?" she asked.

"She had nursery school this morning, then Billie's picking her up. I've got a call into a service about a temporary nanny."

"Anything else I can do to help, let me know."

"I will, if my daughter has any say in it," he replied, moving a few paces toward her. "About every third word out of Rosalind's mouth is Anne. You seem to have a way with children, too."

"Too?"

He shrugged.

Anne leaned on her elbows. "I'm sure it isn't just me and my charm."

"Oh? What is it then?"

Now was the time, Anne thought. *May as well go ahead and tell him what I was thinking last night.*

"Maybe it's just that Rosalind needs a mother."

He pursed his lips. "Is that your instant diagnosis, based on a few hours' contact with me and my child?"

"Well...I, uh, guess it is." Anne now wished she hadn't opened her mouth.

"And are you volunteering?" His tone was sarcastic.

Admittedly Rosalind's need for a mother was none of Anne's concern. Ben should have told her that. Instead he seemed irritated and determined to take her down a peg. Well, two could play at that game. She was tired of holding her tongue while being subjected to his unreasonable and mean-spirited assumptions. "I might consider volunteering," she said, "if you weren't part of the package."

Ben narrowed his eyes and curled his lip in a slight sneer. "Funny, I thought I had what you seem to like best—membership in the male sex. Not only that, I have a good income. I don't have as much money as Tyler Cunningham—few people do—but I'm considered well-off."

"How nice for you," she said. "Then you should have no trouble finding a woman willing to put up with your obnoxious ways and be a mother to Rosalind."

Ben crossed to her desk and leaned over it. "I think Rosalind's doing fine. She's got a father. We don't need anyone else to complicate our lives."

Anne looked up at him, boldly meeting his eyes. "Is that how you see relationships? As complications? Or have you decided that if you don't love, you can't be hurt again?"

Ben's expression was stormy. "I suggest you stop trying to analyze something you don't know a damn thing about." He turned to leave and she rose to follow him.

"I know about losing someone you love."

Ben halted, then retraced his steps and stood facing her. "You mean when one of your men friends refuses to be part of the fan club? By the way, how does Tyler feel about all the others?"

"There aren't any others and we aren't talking about Tyler, or me. We were discussing you."

"No, *we* weren't. *You* were. And trying to poke your nose into something that's none of your affair. Something you can't possibly understand." Ben raised his hands in frustration. "If you're such an expert on wedded bliss, why don't I see a ring on your finger?" He grasped her hand and dropped it just as quickly.

His suggestion stung. Anne had taken off her wedding band after David's funeral, determined to get on with her life. Yet, even now, she felt a little guilty about removing it.

"If you'd ever shown any interest, I might have told you. I understand a great deal about marriage. And I can probably give you a run for your money on the pain of losing someone you love." She leaned against the wall and stared up at the ceiling. "I was a bride before I was eighteen and a mother before I was nineteen." She turned back to Ben. "While I was trying to cope with infant twins, my husband's plane went down in some godforsaken country half a world away."

"I'm sorry." He looked chastened for a moment, but then the challenge returned to his voice. "Yet you never remarried? Didn't *your* children need two parents?"

She shook her head. "My situation was a great deal more complicated than yours. For more than a dozen years I wasn't sure whether I was a wife or a widow."

"And?"

"And then I found out. And I suppose we were fortunate to finally know. A few of the MIAs' remains have been returned, but a lot of families are still in limbo."

"I'm sure it was pretty rough." Ben frowned as he appeared to be making mental calculations. "You couldn't have been married very long when your husband left."

"Less than a year. David's tour began before our first anniversary."

"I'm sorry. But you'll have to agree that's hardly sufficient time to make you much of an expert. If that was your only experience, then you know nothing about marriage."

She opened her mouth to protest, but he held up one hand to prevent her. "You know about first love maybe, the honeymoon part, but nothing about the day-to-day reality when disillusionment sets in. Look around you. How many happy marriages do you see?"

"I've seen quite a few. My parents' for one. Tyler and his wife, Eva. Eva was very dear to me. Her death was a great loss."

"But not too painful to stop you from stepping in to comfort the grieving widower."

Anne's cheeks flushed in anger. "I think I was a comfort to him, but not in the way you're insinuating." Her eyes narrowed. "You're being insulting—to Tyler, as well as to me. If you'd given me half a chance, I would have explained my relationship with Tyler Cunningham."

"You don't need to explain. I've seen how you doll yourself up every Thursday, seen his Cadillac come for you, seen the deference Tyler's driver gives you."

"And so you just put two and two together, hmm?"

"It doesn't take a genius."

"One thing's for sure—you're no genius. As far as relationships go, your IQ's not even measurable." Anne's mouth was getting ahead of her good sense, but she'd built a momentum and couldn't stop herself. "The only people you seem to have in your life are Rosalind and Billie. There's no room for anyone else. You probably wouldn't know what to do with a woman, anyway!"

Ben's eyes flashed. His hands shackled her forearms and pulled her to him. Hard unyielding lips pressed against hers. Slowly, almost reluctantly, they softened, probing, teasing, forcing a response from Anne. A response she couldn't withhold. His arms glided around her body, pressing her closer. She was trembling when he finally released her, and his gaze met hers. "I believe I could figure out what to do with one." Not looking back, he left her office, his walk steady and brisk.

Anne stood frozen in place for several moments. She was stunned, both by the intensity of the kiss and her own reaction to it. What had come over her, insulting Ben like that? Without a doubt her boss certainly *did* know what to do with a woman. And how. She ran a finger over her lips—lips still tingling from his forceful kiss—and relived the sensations she'd felt.

Despite the moodiness and irascible disposition he displayed most of the time, Anne had to admit the man held a certain appeal for her. Maybe that was good; at least she knew she still functioned as a woman. Even though she would never love another man as she had David, it probably meant that she was ready to *feel* again, ready to let another man into her life.

If Tyler knew what she was thinking, he would be delighted. He'd been trying to get her involved for years now.

But would he be delighted that the object of her desire was a man who not only disapproved of her, but considered Tyler to be one of Anne's many romantic conquests? No, he'd be less than amused; she felt sure of *that*.

Anne couldn't help wishing Ben had known from the beginning about the family connection. Explaining it now could be awkward—if and when she had to explain. After all, that kiss... It wasn't really a *kiss*—

it was anger. Nothing more. She shouldn't overreact and try to read anything else into it.

She'd planned some changes in her life—starting with becoming an independent woman who had a meaningful career. Logically, another step would be to establish a relationship with a man. But not now; maybe in a year or two. Not while she was still coming to grips with the career part.

"Ms. MARSHALL, may I see you?" Ben beckoned for her from the door of his office later that morning. On the surface, he showed no more emotion than usual, yet Anne felt a definite tension in the atmosphere.

This was it. After asking her to stay only a short while ago, he was going to fire her for impertinence. Well, what could she say? It was her own fault for opening her big mouth. Time to go in and face the music.

She followed him into the office and watched warily as he shut the door and moved behind his desk to take a seat.

"Do you plan on paying *your* new employee's salary?"

"Pardon?"

"Have you been struck deaf, Ms. Marshall? I'm asking you about this new secretary you hired. The employment agency just called."

"Lisa!" Anne had almost forgotten the young woman. *So that's what this was all about.* Ben was irritated because she'd overstepped her bounds and actually had the nerve to hire an employee without his knowledge.

But she was used to handling problems alone. At home. She reminded herself that this was a different situation. Maybe she'd gone too far—again—but it was too late to back down or appear defensive.

"I thought money was no problem since you've continued to overpay me," she said. "You've never taken me up on that voluntary cut to my own paycheck."

"Pull another stunt like this and your pay *will* be cut. Permanently."

"All right, so I stepped out of line. I'm sorry. But you're always busy and Billie had to have some assistance. You said so yourself. Do you want me to tell Lisa we can't use her?"

"Can she type?"

"Of course not. I hired her because she makes great coffee."

"Sarcasm doesn't become you, Ms. Marshall."

"Sorry. But why would I have hired her if she couldn't type? Does this mean she can stay?"

"We'll see how it works out," Ben conceded. "But from now on, Ms. Fix-it, leave the management of the office to me."

"Whatever you say." Anne left his office feeling almost elated. She had finally won a round with Ben. It was a heady feeling. But there was something more. Despite his grumbling, Anne had the impression he was secretly pleased that she'd taken matters into her own hands and relieved him of an extra burden.

THE WHOLE WEEK went well. Ben gave her a special project of her own to work on. Probably more to keep her out of his hair and away from management decisions than for any other reason. But whatever the motive, for the first time she felt like a real architect.

Then the boys came to town for the S.M.U.-Texas football game and her household returned to the familiar turmoil of rambunctious teenagers. Texas had won the game by one point but had been favored by two touchdowns, so the twins had felt like victors even with a losing score. They'd left at noon Sunday, giving Anne time to clean up after them and to get ready for work the next day.

Lisa, the new secretary, arrived Monday morning, bright and eager. She and Billie got along fabulously—with Billie treating her like a granddaughter and Lisa responding good-naturedly to the nonstop nurturing. Anne immediately knew Lisa would be an asset to Weston and Associates. The office was busy, but calm; there were no major deadlines to meet and no crises occurred. Before she knew it, Thursday had arrived, and Anne was off to Tyler's.

"I HAD LUNCH with Ben yesterday. He said you'd met Rosalind." Tyler opened his napkin and laid it across his lap, then raised his eyes to meet Anne's.

"You were a rat not to clue me in," she scolded.

"But, my dear, it didn't occur to me that you thought she was anything other than his daughter. Only after you left did I begin to sense you were on the wrong track."

"You didn't tell him . . ."

"No, I didn't tell him you thought she was his girl-friend. Even though I find it rather amusing." Tyler chuckled.

"For you, maybe," Anne grumbled. "I, for one, would be terribly embarrassed if he found out."

"Well, you weren't the only one barking up the wrong tree. Ben thinks you and I are romantically in-volved."

"How did you find out? He didn't confront you, did he?"

"Ben? Of course not. Nothing as heavy-handed as that. He simply said something about you working out and then called you my protégé." Tyler threw back his head and laughed heartily. "Protégé. That's a euphe-mism if I ever heard one."

"So did you tell him about our relationship?"

"Not yet. I figured telling him is your department. Your problem."

"It's *his* problem."

"Maybe for now, but it could be yours in the long run. He probably won't relish being embarrassed any more than you did. It's not a good idea to mislead the boss."

Anne shrugged.

"So why didn't you tell him?"

She shrugged again.

"Where did the dinner conversation go? I feel like I'm talking to myself."

"I'm sorry, Tyler. Actually I did try to tell him once, but the man was so pigheaded and judgmental, he wouldn't let me get an explanation in. If he's em-barrassed, it'll be his own fault."

"Why do I have the feeling you're not telling me everything? Could it be that it's a lot safer for you if he thinks you're involved with someone?"

"No, that's not it," she said. But now she wondered why she hadn't made a second attempt to set Ben straight.

"Well, how do you feel about your boss?" Tyler passed her the salad. "Do you still dislike him?"

"Dislike him? No. It's more that I don't understand him."

"Do you want to? Ben Weston appears to be very interesting. At least from what I've seen across a business table."

"Tyler, I know what you're up to—you're matchmaking again. It won't work. I don't want a romance, and if I did, I wouldn't want a romance with Ben Weston. Now can we change the subject?"

Tyler only grinned.

ANNE WAS SWITCHING OFF the lights, ready to go upstairs when she heard the doorbell ring. Had Tyler forgotten something? She retraced her path down the steps, pulled back the curtain on the door and peered outside. Ben Weston was standing on her porch.

She quickly opened the door. "What are you doing here? Is Rosalind okay?"

"Rosalind's fine. Sound asleep. And her expensive new baby-sitter probably is, too," he growled. "Your date brought you home early."

Anne shrugged. She didn't know what to say. What *was* Ben doing here?

Whatever the reason, he appeared intent on staying. He walked into the house without waiting for an invitation and proceeded to look around the living room. "I was on my way home from a meeting and thought maybe we could have a cup of coffee."

"It's late," Anne replied. "Don't you have to relieve the sitter?"

"Only ten-thirty. She agreed to stay late."

"Fine," Anne said abruptly. "I'll put on some coffee." She headed toward the kitchen with Ben following.

She made the coffee, concentrating on the routine task to compose herself before turning back to him. He had one arm propped against an upper cabinet, yet his relaxed stance seemed to contradict his facial expression.

"Well?" she said.

"It seems we had an unfinished conversation last week, and I thought...that is, I've been thinking about it...."

"You must have been, if it was last week." Anne smiled, at the same time wondering whether he was referring to the conversation she'd had such difficulty putting out of her mind. In truth, she hadn't succeeded; she'd been thinking about it, too. Did he remember their kiss as vividly as she did?

"I lost my temper when you mentioned Charlotte—my late wife." Ben looked chagrined. "I wasn't myself."

He didn't have to explain that to her. Anne hardly associated the passionate man she'd witnessed that day with the Ben Weston she knew. So why had he come by tonight? she wondered again. Why was it suddenly necessary, after a week, to set her straight? Perhaps he intended to enlighten her about that, too. She poured the coffee and handed him a mug. "Shall we take these into the den?"

A candle was still flickering on the table, giving the room a cozy glow. Anne settled down on one end of the sofa; Ben took the other.

"I know I'm difficult at times, and you've certainly done nothing but try to do a good job. I appreciate your hiring Lisa and being so great with Rosalind. I guess it's because of Rosalind that I've come. I wanted you to know a little about her mother.

"Despite what you seem to think, I'm not pining over my late wife. If anything, by the time she was killed in that automobile accident, I truly hated her." He ran his fingers through his hair. "She almost destroyed me, and she caused a permanent rift between me and my father.

"My father was a hard man—we'd always had a touch-and-go relationship." Ben frowned, his dark eyebrows drawing together. "He warned me not to marry Charlotte. Told me she was bad news. But I was young, headstrong, and I thought I knew what I wanted." He sat for a few moments, sipping his coffee, lost in thought.

"Dad was positive I married her just to spite him, and maybe I did. Like I said, we'd never gotten along well. But after the marriage..." Ben shook his head. "The worst part was that Charlotte turned out to be every bit as rotten as he'd predicted." He shifted on the sofa and, for the first time since he'd started talking, looked at her directly. "I don't know why I'm telling you all this."

"Everyone needs to confide in someone occasionally," Anne said softly.

He glanced at his wristwatch. "It's late and I've taken too much of your time." He set his half-empty cup on the coffee table and stood up. "I'd better be going."

Anne followed him as he walked to the door. "Well, good night," she said, feeling a bit awkward, unsure of the tone she should take.

He paused for a moment, as though he wanted to say more, or stay longer. Finally he said, "Good night," his voice low and uninflected. He left, striding rapidly down the walk.

Anne stared after him, totally perplexed by his visit. What had prompted Ben to drop in, and what had compelled him to share as much of himself as he had?

CHAPTER FIVE

"OH, WE'RE GOING to see a whale, we're going to see a whale, la la la la la, we're going to see a whale," the little girl's voice sang to the tune of "Farmer in the Dell."

Anne got up from behind her drafting table and went into the reception area.

"Anne!" Rosalind squealed. "I've missed you and missed you!" She wrapped her arms around Anne's legs in a hug.

"I've missed you, too," Anne said, picking up the child for a quick kiss on the cheek before returning her to the floor. "What are you doing here today?"

"Billie picked me up at school and brought me. Daddy's going to leave work early and we're going to see..." She broke into song again. "Oh, we're going to see a whale."

"San Antonio," Ben explained, coming out of his office, as if Anne hadn't already guessed where he and Rosalind were headed. This was the first time Anne had seen him today and she was caught off guard. He wasn't in his typical work uniform of suit and tie; instead he wore a blue broadcloth shirt, jeans and a beige sport coat with leather patches on the elbows. Anne's heart gave a little flutter. She quickly excused the sensation. Any woman would have reacted the same way. Ben looked devastating—sexy, rugged and dangerously male. Not at all like the dispassionate businessman she usually saw.

"Daddy, can Anne come with us? Please?" Rosalind begged.

Anne didn't know what to say. She was certain Ben didn't want her along. "I don't think your daddy's car will hold me, too," she told Rosalind before Ben had a chance to answer. It was an excuse that should seem plausible to the little girl.

"We could take your car—it's big." Rosalind pulled on her father's arm. "Couldn't we, Daddy?"

Again, Anne gave him no time to reply. "I'm sorry, Rosalind, but I'm not the boss like your daddy. He can leave, but I have to stay here and work."

"Daddy will let you come if you ask him nice and say please."

Anne lifted her hands in supplication to Ben; he'd have to deal with this.

"Maybe Anne doesn't want to come, Rosalind," he said gently.

"Yes, she does. Everyone likes whales. You want to come, don't you, Anne?"

Anne glanced self-consciously around the reception area as she noticed all the attention directed their way. Billie and Lisa had stopped typing to stare at them. Willie and Hank were frozen in place on their way out the front door, apparently more intent on hearing what would happen than in going to lunch. Even Mason had stopped midway up the stairs as if poised to learn Anne's answer. The scene was down-right embarrassing.

"Of course I want to come, Rosalind. But I can't today."

Rosie's thumb went into her mouth, and she seemed close to tears.

"I think the work can wait, don't you Anne?" Ben said. "I doubt Rosalind could enjoy the outing knowing you were here missing the fun."

The little girl's thumb eased from her mouth, as her eyes flashed Anne a conspiratorial look.

The little demon, Anne thought. *She's playing her daddy like a well-tuned guitar.* It was definitely time for the adults to concede defeat. "Well, we can't have Rosalind not enjoying the show, now can we? Let me get my purse."

The three of them headed toward Anne's station wagon. As they stepped in front of the car, she asked Ben, "Would you mind if we run by my place? It's a little out of the way, but I'd be a lot more comfort-able in a pair of slacks and some low-heeled shoes."

"We don't mind, do we, Daddy? I could say hello to Fred and Ginger and Frank." She looked up at Anne. "Has Ginger had her puppies yet?"

"Not yet," Anne told her, "but any day now."

"Will you tell Daddy so he can bring me to see them?"

Anne nodded. "I sure will."

"Why don't we follow you?" Ben suggested. "Then we won't have to come back by the office for my car."

"Fine," Anne said.

"Fine," Rosalind echoed. "Can I ride with Anne?"

Once again, Anne was at a loss for words. She didn't want to intrude on this father-daughter outing, but she didn't want to reject the child, either.

Ben handled it for her. "Okay, you can go with Anne, but keep your seat belt fastened." He turned to Anne. "Sometimes she undoes it," he explained.

Anne had to give him credit. While he was often reclusive and uncommunicative at work, to Rosalind he was a kind, devoted father. Surprisingly, however, the knowledge was more disturbing than satisfying. Anne was finding herself increasingly attracted to Ben and she wished she weren't. Despite his slight softening, she doubted there was a place in his life for a woman. And if there were? Somehow, that was even more threatening. She wasn't ready for a relationship with anyone yet. Especially not with Ben Weston.

An hour later the three were on their way to San Antonio. The eighty-mile trip was one of Anne's favorite outings. It was especially nice being able to concentrate on the scenery—Ben had volunteered to drive. Because the water park was relatively new, she and the boys had never gone there, but they'd often visited other San Antonio attractions: the Alamo, the zoo and some of the old missions.

The boys never tired of the Alamo and Anne sometimes felt as if she could hold her own with the Daughters of the Republic of Texas, the women who oversaw the day-to-day operation of the old chapel-fortress. She could describe in detail the famous battle and relate the exploits of Jim Bowie and William Travis, commanders during the siege.

Of course, the Daughters didn't have to witness daily reenactments as she did when Jody and James assumed the roles of the fallen heroes. Both boys still had replicas of Davy Crockett's coonskin hat dangling from coatracks in their rooms. And if they'd shouted ''Remember the Alamo'' once, they must have done it a thousand times. She sighed, reflecting that those days were gone forever, then turned around to look at Rosalind.

Rosalind was sitting in the back seat, chattering happily to her stuffed bear about Anne's animals. It was a shame she couldn't have a pet, Anne thought. She obviously loved cats and dogs.

Anne turned her eyes from the back seat to look at Ben. ''Have you heard anything from Mrs. Schneider?''

''Yes,'' Ben answered. ''She sent a note—her sister's a lot better, but she's going to be needed in Germany for a while yet. Good thing I found a temporary sitter.''

Ben eased the station wagon into a parking space. ''Perfect timing,'' he said. ''We have fifteen minutes to get to the stadium before the first show starts.''

Rosalind was in total awe when the object of her trip appeared. The animal's performance lived up to its publicity. The huge black-and-white killer whale jumped on cue, gave rides to her trainers, and was as gentle with them as a family pet.

''Daddy, can I have my own whale?''

Anne and Ben laughed. "Well," Ben said, "where would we keep one?"

"In the swimming pool!"

Ben laughed again. "The pool might be a little small... I think I have a better idea."

After the show, the three wandered around the landscaped grounds. Ben carried his daughter's new stuffed whale; Rosalind walked between Anne and Ben, who each held one of her hands. "I'm your little girl today too," she told Anne. "I belong to both of you."

Anne didn't know how to respond to the child. But then, she supposed it wasn't really her role. Surprisingly, Ben didn't seem upset by his daughter's words; in fact, he seemed more mellow than Anne could ever remember. Maybe removing that tie and unbuttoning his collar had allowed some fresh air into those stuffy thoughts of his.

"It's after six," Ben said, "time to be heading home."

Rosalind's mouth turned down in a pout.

Ben laughed. "Might as well smile, Rosie. We're leaving either way. We'll stop somewhere and eat dinner." He started toward the parking-lot shuttle bus.

Rosie acquiesced good-naturedly and, still positioned between the two adults, started swinging her arms back and forth. Anne's and Ben's arms went up and down keeping pace with the child's rhythm.

"That was fun," Rosie said, once the shuttle trip was completed and she was settled in the car. "Did you ever come here with your big boys, Anne?"

Anne turned around. "No, but I think they've visited with their girlfriends."

"Oh . . . I was hoping maybe I could be their girlfriend. What're their names?"

"James and Jody," Anne said. "And I'm sure they'd like you to be one of their girlfriends. They make nice boyfriends—they call and send flowers." She shot a pointed look at Ben.

"Okay," Rosalind agreed. "I'm hungry. And after we eat, we can see Fred and Ginger and Frank."

"You'll probably be too tired," Ben said. Anne noted a twinkle in his eyes that reminded her of Rosie.

"No, I won't," Rosalind protested. "I'm not tired at all. You'll see, I won't be a bit tired." They rode along quietly for a few more miles. Then Ben glanced in the rearview mirror and laughed. "Take a look."

Rosie had put her Winnie-the-Pooh against the window and nestled her head against the cuddly toy. She was sound asleep, her arms curled around the stuffed black-and-white whale.

"She's a good child," Anne said, glancing in the back seat. "And you're a good father."

Ben shrugged. "I'm lucky to have her. It's hard to imagine a life without Rosalind." His eyes took on a distant look and for a moment Anne thought he was going to say something else, but he remained silent.

"I feel the same way," she said. "The boys have always brought me such joy."

"You miss them?"

"Yes, all the time. Still, there are compensations for their being older."

"Like?"

"Like knowing they're able to take care of themselves now. I worried so much—what if something happened to me, what would they do?" Anne knew Tyler would have stepped in, of course, but how could she explain that to Ben? This simply wasn't the right time to launch into the whole complicated situation.

"I know what you mean. I'm the only family Rosalind has. Her mother and I were both only children, and all the grandparents are gone." He looked as though he might say more, but he seemed to think better of it and said nothing else.

Anne was surprised to discover she'd dozed off just like Rosie; the next thing she knew they were pulling up outside a Mexican restaurant in Austin.

"This all right?" Ben asked. "Rosie and I like the food here."

Anne nodded in agreement at his choice. She pulled her comb out of her purse and ran it through her hair. "Do I look okay?"

"You look fine," Ben said. "Maybe a little sunburned across the nose, but otherwise, just fine."

Anne pulled out a compact, powdered her nose and refreshed her lipstick. Sure enough, despite the sunscreen she'd worn, there was a hint of red across her nose. Her fair skin had always been sensitive.

They started off with frozen margaritas topped off by a trickle of sangria, while Rosalind had a Shirley Temple. Then all three dined on chicken *fajitas*—strips of grilled chicken breast wrapped in flour tortillas and garnished with lettuce, tomato and shredded cheddar cheese. Rosalind's nap had revived her and again she chatted away, dominating the conversation. Anne was relieved, because there seemed to be a subtle change in her relationship with Ben, a new awareness that made her even more uncomfortable in his presence.

"How did you get Fred and Ginger and Frank?" Rosalind asked.

"James and Jody rescued Frank from the animal shelter, and Fred and Ginger were a gift from Tyler Cunningham. He's..."

"A friend of Anne's," Ben finished for her. His voice lowered and he moved closer to Anne as he spoke. "I'm surprised you've managed to get through a day without mentioning Tyler, but obviously you've thought of him. I've got to hand it to him—giving a pet. Such a clever idea. Keeps you in the person's mind forever."

"You're being offensive." Anne's voice was also an angry whisper. "It's nothing unusual for a—"

"Are you mad at each other?" Rosalind looked concerned. She'd immediately noticed the tension. She might be young, but her intuition was well developed.

"Of course not," Ben answered. "We were just discussing a problem from the office." He drew out his wallet and dropped a bill on the table to cover the check. "Now let's go see the animals."

"Goody!" Rosalind said, easily distracted. She skipped in front of them, but stopped at the door, her eyes focusing on the two adults.

Anne was walking several steps in front of Ben, her lips pursed in indignation, while Ben had assumed his formal guarded demeanor.

"Are you *sure* you're not mad?" Rosalind asked again.

"Of course we're not mad," Ben answered. "I'm not mad. Are you mad, Anne?"

What could she say? Anne didn't want to worry the child. "No, I'm not mad, Rosie." Actually it was easier just to stay angry and continue the misconception about Tyler than to tell Ben the truth and acknowledge the growing chemistry between them. Ben was changing. The way he looked at her, the way he talked to her—it made her nervous.

"See." Ben smiled at the little girl, then unexpectedly draped an arm around Anne as they walked toward the car.

"That's better," Rosalind said. "We're like a family again."

As the child raced ahead of them, Anne tried to shrug out of Ben's hold, but he pulled her back to him.

"Stop that. You're just encouraging her to—"

"To what?"

"To fantasize that this outing is something more than it is."

"And what is it?"

"Just an employee going along at the invitation of a child. Nothing more."

"Nothing? I stand corrected." Ben removed his arm.

Now Anne felt miserable. With Ben she always seemed to say the wrong thing. She couldn't win.

FRED'S BARK MET THEM in the yard when they arrived at Anne's. "Something's wrong," she said. "He sounds different." She rushed toward the house, leaving the back door open for Ben and Rosalind to follow.

There in her basket with five tiny puppies was Ginger, wagging her tail proudly. "Rosalind, come over here," Anne said quietly. "Look what we have."

As Ben hovered, Rosalind crouched by the basket. "Look Daddy. Oooh, they're darlink. Just darlink." Anne and Ben glanced at one another over her head and chuckled. *Darlink?*

"Are you okay, old girl?" Anne examined the dog, while Fred plopped down by the basket, wearing a doggy grin. "He looks as if he is ready to pass out dog biscuits to the other animals in the neighborhood, don't you think?" she said playfully to Rosalind. "Would you like to get him a treat? In the bottom cupboard there. One for Ginger, too."

The child leapt up to collect the biscuits and Anne glanced over at Ben. "Do you care for a glass of wine or some brandy?"

"I don't think so," Ben said. "It's getting late, and Rosie's had a lot of excitement today. We'd better be getting on home."

"Just a minute more, pleeeze, Daddy. Look, Ginger lets me hold them." She nestled a tiny puppy in her lap. "This is Debbie. And that one's Gene, this one's Donald, and this one's—"

"Whoa, Rosalind. The puppies belong to Anne— we'd better let her name them."

"But they're all dancers. I saw them dance in a movie. Mrs. Schneider and I watched it two times. She likes movies with dancing. Fred and Ginger are dancers, too, aren't they, Anne?"

"So they are. But we need to check to make sure we give them the right names, boy names and girl names, don't you think?"

"And to think up some more dancers' names, right?"

"Right," Anne agreed.

"Are you going to call James and Jody?" Rosalind asked as she and Ben were leaving.

Anne laughed. "I suppose I'd better. Thanks for reminding me."

"Well, we'll say good-night then." Ben nudged Rosalind toward the door and Anne bent quickly to kiss her on the cheek.

When she rose, Anne met Ben's eyes head-on. His look was sending a message as old as time, but she wasn't sure how to answer. She was drawn to him, *wanted* his lips on hers. And she knew he felt the same way. It wasn't the first time she'd sensed this sympathetic communication between them. She felt bewildered.

Ben solved her dilemma by leaning over and kissing her on the forehead. "Good night, Anne. Thanks for spending today with us."

ANNE DIDN'T KNOW what she expected the next day at work, but it was...different. That was the only way to describe the subtly changed atmosphere. An unspoken question hovered over the office like morning mist, yet none of her coworkers asked what Anne

knew was on each of their minds. Billie and Lisa said
nothing, but the inquiry in their eyes was unmistak-
able. Willie asked how the trip was. Anne responded
truthfully that it was fun and that he should take his
family to the water park if they hadn't already been.
Mason made a suggestive comment about her "over-
time with the boss," which Anne ignored. The man in
question didn't show up at the office until almost
eleven; his baby-sitter had quit and he'd had to line up
a new one.

"Hi, how's the new family?" He was leaning casually against her office door, his navy blazer slung
over one shoulder, yet his nonchalant pose seemed a
little contrived. Anne sensed that his innate defen-
siveness had returned. It was something in his eyes, his
voice. Something that said *Don't read anything into
yesterday. It meant nothing.*

Well, she could play that game, too; she could be
just as nonchalant as Ben. "Mother and babies are
fine. Thanks for asking. Did you find a new sitter?"

"I'm interviewing one later on today. Listen, Hank
is heading up to Temple to check out a proposed site
for one of our new clients. A small retail center.
Thought you might like to go with him."

Anne nodded. "Sure." Ben had been giving her
more responsible assignments since Lisa had come,
but she viewed this offer primarily as a way to get her
out of the office. Obviously he'd had enough of her
company yesterday.

Anne and Hank made the trip, decided the site was
perfect, and spent the next day conferring with the
client. Then it was quitting time and Anne was

shocked by how quickly the day had gone. It was also Thursday. Tyler himself was picking her up from work.

She was just closing the gate behind her as he drove up. He got out of the car and kissed her on the cheek, then opened the passenger door for her. Anne turned and looked back when she'd climbed in. Ben was watching them. Tyler also noticed Ben on the porch and waved; the wave was halfheartedly returned. Then Ben swung around and went back into the building.

"If I didn't know better, I'd say I've been snubbed," Tyler said.

Anne didn't answer.

"Looks like the young man has a serious case of jealousy."

"Nonsense. He's just got a lot on his mind. Now, are we going to see the puppies, or aren't we?"

Tyler slid behind the wheel. "We'll check on them, then I'm taking you out to dinner for a change. Hannah's on a well-deserved vacation."

Anne was pleased to hear the evening's plans. While she always enjoyed eating at Tyler's home, she thought it a good sign that he was getting out more. He had spent so many reclusive years nursing Eva through her illness. Anne knew the forced confinement must have been difficult for the sociable Tyler. She wondered if he might consider dating again—or even marriage. *Stop that,* she told herself. *You're becoming as meddlesome as Tyler.* Yet, for some reason, she'd thought a lot about marriage lately.

After a brief stop to admire the puppies, they dined at a barbecue place west of the city, then returned to her house for coffee. Tyler sat at the breakfast table watching her put the fluted paper filter into the coffee basket and measure out grounds. "Anne, you still haven't told Ben about us. Why?"

"I've tried—several times." *But not very hard,* she admitted to herself. "Something always comes up and I can never get it out. I don't know what to do about him." She poured water into the top of the coffee maker.

"Do you *want* to do something about him?"

"Stop trying to make a relationship between Ben and me. You're just as bad as he is, jumping to conclusions." Anne placed the sugar bowl and creamer on the table in front of Tyler.

He touched her arm, gazing steadily into her eyes. "I only want you to be happy, Anne. You need someone in your life."

"I have someone. Several someones. James and Jody and you... And now a houseful of puppies." She moved to the cabinet and returned with cups. "Actually you're the one who could use some company," Anne said, forgetting her earlier resolve to leave Tyler's social life alone. "You're a handsome eligible bachelor."

"We're talking about your love life, not mine," he replied gruffly.

"I don't have a love life." Anne picked up the now full coffee carafe and carried it to the table.

"Then you should. Ben's obviously attracted to you."

"I doubt that, but it hardly matters, anyway. I'm not attracted to him." She kept her voice brisk and no-

nonsense, hoping Tyler would accept this as her last word on the subject. For tonight, anyway.

"Oh, Anne, what am I going to do with you?" He laughed and shook his head. "I give up." He poured cream into his coffee. "So tell me, are the boys coming home this weekend?"

"Do you think I could keep them away? I'm surprised they didn't cut class and drive down as soon as I called. Sometimes you'd think those two were eight instead of eighteen. They can't wait to spoil the new pups. Made me promise not to name them, although truthfully I've been calling them the names Rosalind gave them." She realized as she spoke that she'd brought Ben and Rosalind back into the conversation, although it was the very thing she'd been determined not to do. Strange how often they came into her thoughts, how easily they'd become part of her existence.

"Has Rosie been over to see them again?"

"Not yet, but she'll probably be here sometime during the weekend. Ben can't seem to resist her pleas for too long."

"What do you imagine the boys will think of your new little friend?"

Anne hadn't considered it. She hoped Ben and Rosie didn't stop in when James and Jody were home. She was having enough trouble with Tyler; she didn't want to have to field the boys' questions, too.

AN HOUR LATER Anne had let the animals outside and stood waiting at the kitchen door for Ginger when the twin beams of a car's headlights flashed in the driveway. Ben got out and walked to the door.

"May I come in, Anne? For coffee?"

"It's cold, but I can make more," she said, moving back into the kitchen. Ben followed her, Ginger trotting along behind.

Ben crouched on the floor by Ginger's basket and played with the puppies while Anne brewed another pot of coffee—decaffeinated this time. She leaned against the counter watching him, while the automatic pot dripped in the background. Despite his apparent interest in the animals, Ben looked preoccupied. And annoyed. She wondered why he'd dropped by again.

After she'd taken more china from the cabinet and set a tray with cups and saucers, teaspoons, the jug of cream and sugar bowl, Ben left the animals and joined her, lifting the tray from her hands and carrying it to the living room. They sat side by side on the sofa, almost like two strangers, neither venturing any conversation.

Finally Anne could tolerate the silence no longer. "Why are you here, Ben? Is there a problem?"

Ben sipped his coffee, then set the cup and saucer on the table. He leaned forward, his long artistic hands clasped between his knees. "You—you're the problem. I just don't understand you. You come across like Miss Goody Two Shoes...Professional Widow... Earth Mother. Then carry on with a man old enough to be your father!"

"I don't believe what I'm hearing! Did you come over here in the middle of the night to lecture me on morality?"

Ben scowled. "It's hardly the middle of the night. Frankly, I'm surprised Tyler's gone. But I suppose at his age he can't handle too many late evenings."

"I'm sick of your ridiculous assumptions! This is the last straw. Tyler Cunningham is my father-in-law! *Father-in-law.* Can you get that through your head?"

There was a long silence as Ben frowned, obviously reflecting on her words. "Tyler and I have been closely associated for a long time—why haven't I ever heard about you? Besides, your name isn't Cunningham."

"You don't believe me? Obviously, you don't know Tyler as well as you think!" She forced herself to speak more calmly. "Maybe because you've had primarily a business relationship. Tyler hasn't socialized much the past few years, what with Eva's illness and all. I see him a lot because he's family. He was David's stepfather, but the love between them was as strong as any father and son I've ever known."

She saw a look of sadness pass over Ben's face. Was he remembering his relationship with his own father? But he recovered quickly. "So that explains the name."

"That explains the name. Now is that all you want?"

He moved closer to Anne. "All? No, not all." His face was drawn, almost frozen in anger. "I want to know why you felt it necessary to mislead me." His expression softened. "And I want this..." He grasped her arms and pulled her against his chest. Then fiercely, his lips bore down on hers and his arms encircled her.

She tried to push him away, but was powerless in the grip of his embrace. The cool and collected Bennett Weston had disappeared and now this other man—this other Ben—was crushing her body and her lips. She felt desire begin to well up as her lips parted under his, her entire body flushed with a passion unspent for years.

The emotion was so new, so strange, it caught her off guard and frightened her. Finally when his lips slid down to her neck, she found the strength to utter a hoarse "No."

"Do you really mean that?" he whispered.

"I mean it," she said, her voice uneven.

For a moment she thought he was going to object, but instead he loosened his embrace. "I don't think you do," he countered, then rose and walked out the door, leaving Anne sitting alone, her fingers on her swollen lips.

CHAPTER SIX

"WHY?" ANNE ASKED Ginger, while opening a can of frozen orange juice. "Why?"

The Lab was lying in her basket, trapped by the nursing litter, as Anne voiced her frustrations about Ben's unexpected visit. Fred was out chasing squirrels in the yard, and Anne knew Ginger was ready to be relieved of her motherly duties, anxious to be out playing, too. But the puppies were still too small to be left alone. So the dog had to endure both her demanding pups and her mistress's tirade.

But much as she tried to dismiss Ben's visit as simple contrariness, her memories of the night before were too vivid. She could feel his arms around her, the touch of his mouth against hers. How would he act today? She felt tempted to call in sick—she wasn't ready to face him yet.

FACING BEN didn't turn out to be a problem. He wasn't in the office when she arrived. "The boss fired the new sitter. He's interviewing again," Billie informed her.

Billie left early that afternoon and three of the other architects were also out. Only Hank Gonzalez kept Anne company during the late afternoon. He was upstairs working at his drafting table, while Anne answered some routine correspondence. The office was already locked and she had just finished the last letter when she heard the outer door open.

Ben stuck his head into her office. "I'd like to see you for a few minutes before you go."

Anne nodded. She sorted the work she was taking with her and packed her briefcase. Clutching it in one hand and her purse in the other, she stopped at Ben's office. She wanted to emphasize that she only had a moment to spare.

He looked up and gestured for her to come closer. "I was a little out of line last night. How about dinner tomorrow so I can make amends?"

She regarded him skeptically. She had the impression there was some hidden agenda here. "I don't think so."

"Anne..." His eyes were stormy, as though she'd angered him by refusing, but then his voice softened. "Perhaps some other time."

"Perhaps."

All the way home Anne fretted over Ben's invitation. She *was* right to say no—she certainly didn't need any more involvement. She wished she could rationalize why Ben seemed to have done a 180-degree turn in his attitude toward her. It wasn't learning about Tyler, because he'd started changing before that; he'd been different ever since the dinner at her house with Rosalind. Rosalind... Could she have been the catalyst? Anne couldn't help wondering whether Ben was suddenly attracted to her for herself or because his daughter liked her. Whichever, she needed to get everything back on a strictly business footing with her boss. Unfortunately they seemed to have moved beyond that, and Ben was on her mind entirely too much. She felt like a schoolgirl again—experiencing sensations she no longer knew how to handle. Thank goodness the twins were coming home for the weekend. Their presence would hasten a much-needed return to reality.

"HEY, MOM, we're out of bread and cheese and smoked turkey. And you'd better get some more chips and soft drinks, too. Some of the gang are coming over later." James was hunched over the refrigerator—a usual position for him—peering in. Jody was in the backyard tossing a stick for Fred.

Anne, after a leisurely Saturday morning with her sons, was getting dressed. She sat down in a kitchen chair and pulled on socks and a pair of running shoes. "Just add it to the list on the cabinet," she said, shaking her head. "I'd have to take out a loan if you two came home very often."

"You know you love having us here, Mumsey."

"Well, maybe I do."

"Good, so will you prove it by baking a German chocolate cake later?"

"Did I hear something about cake?" Jody let the screen door bang shut and flopped into the recliner, fanning himself with the newspaper. "Old Fred's not getting enough exercise. He gave out before I did. He's underneath the oleander bush, panting away." Jody glanced out the window. "Now he's running to the front gate—looks like we have company."

Anne tied her shoes and rushed to the door. Could it be...? She could see two figures through the curtain. It *was* Rosalind, but she was accompanied by Billie, not Ben.

"Good morning, Anne," Billie said. "I hope you don't mind our just dropping by, but we were in the neighborhood and Rosie insisted we had to stop and see the puppies."

"Not at all. Come on inside." Anne ushered them to the kitchen. "Billie, meet my sons James and Jody." The boys stood up. "This is Billie Potter and Rosalind Weston—Rosie."

Rosie launched herself at the boys. "Hello, I've been wanting and wanting to meet you. Anne said I could be your girlfriend."

"Sure," the boys agreed, casting Anne a glance of bewilderment.

Rosalind then ran to Ginger's basket. "Hello, Donald and Gene. And this is Debbie, *my* dog. Have you named the others, Anne?"

Anne was surprised Rosalind remembered the three she'd named, but she had. How was Ben going to tell her she couldn't have one? Well, that was his problem. Anne wanted Rosalind to have Debbie, as much as Rosalind wanted the puppy. "Yes, this one's Misha, after Mikhail Baryshnikov, and this one's Rudy, after Rudolf Nureyev. There was only one girl in the whole litter."

"Then I'll take Misha, if you want to keep Debbie. I love them both. I love them all!" Rosalind kissed the puppy she was holding.

Billie and Anne chatted with the boys for a few minutes, Billie asking the usual questions about school and how they liked the Dallas-Fort Worth area. James and Jody answered politely, while holding back the questions Anne could see in their eyes.

"Come, Rosie. We've got to be going," Billie said.

Rosalind made no protest, but gave Anne and both boys a hug before she trotted out to the car. "Daddy and I will come back," she shouted as Billie joined her.

Anne closed the door, then crossed to the kitchen cabinet to pick up her grocery list and car keys.

"Wait a minute, Mumsey," James said. "Just *who* is Rosalind? And, more important, *who* is 'Daddy'? Seems there's something you haven't told us."

Anne erased all emotion from her face as she looked at her son. "'Daddy' is my boss, Bennett Weston, and Billie's his secretary. I've been talking about the animals at work and Rosalind just had to see them." She headed for her car, the boys at her heels.

"Then how come she'd already named three of them?" Jody asked, "and why is one of the pups hers?"

"You know what children are like," Anne replied. She got into the car without volunteering anything else. As she backed out of the driveway, she watched the boys in the rearview mirror. "And I know what *my* children are like," she muttered. "Those two aren't going to let me off the hook this easily.

THE PHONE WAS RINGING as Anne arrived home one evening the following week. She'd been out to dinner with Molly Wilson, an old friend from high school who had moved away and was back in town for a business meeting. Molly—a former divorcée—spent the entire time talking animatedly about her new husband, a man she'd married a few months ago.

Even though Anne felt genuinely happy for her friend, she couldn't suppress a twinge of envy. She was more aware than ever before of how confusing man-woman relationships could be. She wished she could feel as hopeful and optimistic as Molly. But she couldn't, and Molly's happiness only served to make her more depressed.

She'd wanted to talk to Molly about Ben, wanted to share her uncertainties with a friend. But what could she really say? She didn't understand the situation well enough to discuss it, even with an old pal like Molly. Maybe because her emotions were too new, too intangible to be explained.

She hurriedly unlocked the back door, then closed it behind her as she rushed to answer the ringing phone, almost breathless with her "Hello."

"You've been out?" said Ben.

"Yes," she answered, not offering more information.

"With Tyler?"

"No. I occasionally see someone other than Tyler."

"Of course." His voice was controlled, yet Anne felt she could detect a hint of displeasure.

For a moment both were silent.

"Why did you call, Ben?"

Another moment passed. "If you're not busy tomorrow, how about having dinner with me?"

"I don't think so."

"Why not?" The annoyance was obvious now.

"It wouldn't be a good idea. You're the one who cautioned me about interoffice relationships."

"Anne—"

"I'm too tired to talk now, Ben. I'll see you in the morning." She hung up the phone. Hung up on him was more like it, she thought ruefully, but the phone didn't ring again. Maybe she hadn't handled the situation very wisely, but something in Anne's subconscious told her she shouldn't go out with Ben Weston. It was too much of a risk.

"WHAT'S GOT INTO BEN? You two have a fight?" Mason was perched on the front of her desk, examining his fingernails as he waited for her answer. Anne didn't want to answer his nosy question—actually, all she wanted was the power to make him disappear. She could understand why Ben kept Mason on his staff; he was not only a talented architect but skillful in dealing with clients. But she still didn't like him. Her initial impressions hadn't changed. The man was a boor.

"Can't either of you find anything to do?" Ben was standing at the door, a cup of coffee in his hand, glaring at them.

Mason shrugged and rose from his half-sitting position. "Sorry, boss." He grinned, leaving the office.

"Did you need something?" Anne's voice was businesslike, even though she felt like screaming. Ben Weston was the most exasperating man she'd ever met, so unpredictable that she never knew where she stood with him.

"No," he replied. "Nothing at all." He turned abruptly and went back to his own office.

So this was how things were going to be. Well, that was fine with her. If he was waiting for an apology, he'd have a long wait. Anyway, she'd done nothing to apologize for. Her decision had been the right one; his erratic ways disturbed her equilibrium almost as much as her unexpected attraction to him did.

Her relationship with Ben outside the office had taken a direction she found hard to contend with. His self-righteous anger at least gave her some breathing room. Maybe he'd sulk for weeks, she thought hopefully, and leave her alone with her safe dependable routine. Work and home and family—what more did she need?

TYLER WAS SITTING in his long white sedan when Anne left work at the end of the day.

"Hello," she said halfheartedly as she got into the car.

"Hello yourself," Tyler said, eyeing her warily. "What's up?"

She didn't answer.

"Nice day," he said. "Starting to cool off a bit."

"If you say so."

"Why are you in such a miserable mood? I'd have had Red pick you up if I'd known you were going to be so down in the mouth."

"It's just been a bad day. I'll be okay."

Tyler swung the car away from the curb. "I understand my good reputation's been restored," he teased.

Anne shrugged, then took off her sunglasses and tucked them in her purse. Daylight saving time had ended and it was getting dark earlier. Even the white limestone cliffs framing the road toward Land's End seemed duller in the autumn night.

Tyler chuckled. "I also understand Ben asked you out."

"Is there no privacy anymore? Are you two starting a dialogue about me?" she asked sharply, turning to face him.

"Of course not. I called him for a dinner appointment tomorrow and he said he hoped to be taking my daughter-in-law out. Is he?"

"No."

"Anne, I think you should reconsider. Ben seems like the kind of man who would be good for you."

"I have no intention of reconsidering. Now can we please change the subject? What're you doing for Thanksgiving?"

Tyler gave her a look of frustration, then answered, "Thought you might all like to come to Land's End. Hannah's planning a big feast, and the Cowboys game will be on."

Like turkey and dressing, football was almost synonymous with Thanksgiving Day in Texas. The Dallas Cowboys had a winning season so far, and it looked like they might even be headed for the Super Bowl.

"Then we'd better plan the meal around the game," Anne said.

"When are the boys coming home?"

"Wednesday night, and I'm sure they'd love to come to Land's End. Would Hannah like me to bring something? Maybe a couple of pumpkin pies? Or pecan?"

"I'll check with her and let you know next week."

The conversation turned back to James and Jody, and Anne escaped further query concerning Ben.

ANNE WAS READY FOR BED, dressed in pink pajamas, when the doorbell rang and Fred started barking. She reached into the closet for her matching robe and a pair of slippers, then hurried downstairs.

"Who could it be at this hour?" she asked the Lab, who was poised at the foot of the stairs barking furiously. "Surely *you-know-who* wouldn't have the nerve to come here again," she muttered to herself.

She glimpsed the solitary figure through the front door curtains. It *was* Ben. She patted the dog's head. "It's okay, boy." Was there no limit to his persistence? she wondered. Yet her body belied her supposed irritation: her pulse had accelerated and she felt a warm rush of excitement in spite of her apprehensions.

She opened the door as far as the safety chain would permit. "Ben, is something wrong?"

He held up a bottle of wine. "I brought a peace offering. I hoped we might have a drink."

"We're not at war and, besides, it's too late."

He looked at his watch. "It's only half past nine. Surely you weren't asleep this early." He paused, taking in her nighttime attire through the crack in the door.

What was he up to now? With Ben Weston, how was she ever to know? One thing was for sure: these late-night visits were becoming a habit—a habit that seemed out of character for him. But then, she supposed she couldn't be certain of that. Because, in reality, she didn't know Ben very well yet. The different sides he presented hadn't yet meshed into a coherent whole—the self-contained autocrat at work, the indulgent parent with Rosalind, and the enigmatic male the rest of the time.

She released the chain and pulled the door open all the way. "Come on in."

"Finally." His voice had a tone of sarcastic belligerence, which subsided as he said, "Lead on to the kitchen."

Anne thought she detected a hint of seduction in his manner. The idea seemed implausible, yet he had kissed her before—on more than one occasion. She shrugged and headed for the kitchen, Ben following closely behind.

She handed him a corkscrew and, while he opened the bottle, Anne took two stemmed glasses from the cabinet.

"Shall we sit in the living room?" Ben passed her a glass of wine.

"I should go up and change—I'm really not dressed for company," she protested.

"You look fine to me. Beautiful, in fact."

Beautiful? Anne wondered how long it had been since Ben had said anything that complimentary to a woman. Why was he suddenly given to outrageous flattery? And that's what it was. No one could think her beautiful now; she'd already removed her make-up, and her robe and pajamas were anything but glamorous. What *was* the man up to?

"Why did you come?" Might as well get to the point of his visit, she decided. She was seated at one end of the floral chintz couch in her living room, fin-gering the stem of her glass. Ben was at the other end, his jacket off, the sleeves of his white shirt rolled to the elbows.

"To see you, of course. Does that surprise you? I want to spend some time with you, but you keep re-fusing my dinner invitations, so..." He shifted closer to her, his arm resting on the back of the sofa. His hand touched her shoulder.

"You're making me uncomfortable."

"What can I do to make you more comfortable? I thought I sensed something between us."

"You sensed wrong."

"Are you certain?" His knuckles gently stroked a path across her cheek.

She rose from the couch and went to stand by the fireplace. "You don't understand."

Ben was right behind her. "Then help me." He put his arms around her. "Help me understand," he said, urging her closer. His lips on hers silenced any reply.

Try as she might to deny any feelings, her body was sending a different message. The kiss went on for long moments before Anne could bring herself to push him away.

She gazed into his eyes. They had a fire she'd never seen in them before, a glow she recognized as passion. That feeling of unrest came over her again, and she knew she had to free herself before she became hopelessly ensnared in his spell.

"It's late, Ben."

For a moment she thought he was going to argue. Instead he picked up his suit jacket from the back of a chair, gave a sigh of resignation, then headed to the front door. "Good night, Anne," he said softly, shutting the door behind him.

Anne collected the two wineglasses and returned to the kitchen. She stood in the empty room, sipping the remaining wine in her glass, trying to make some sense of Ben's behavior. And her own. But she was too confused to analyze anything at the moment. She sighed, just as Ben had, and made her way upstairs.

Ben was apparently determined to continue with his romantic pursuit. A flower van was parked in her driveway when she drove in from work the next day and an exquisite arrangement of cut flowers handed to her by the delivery boy. As soon as she got inside, the phone rang—it was Ben asking her to dinner again. When she refused, he was amiable about it and didn't press her, but the next afternoon, he appeared in her office with Rosalind. The little girl was much more difficult to turn down than her father, and Anne found herself up early on Saturday morning preparing for a trip to the movies with them to see a new children's feature.

Ben and Rosalind arrived at Anne's house shortly after noon; Rosalind gave Anne a hug, then went straight to the puppies. "Mrs. Schneider's staying in Germany, so that means I can have a dog now," she told Anne happily.

Ben groaned. "I spent half the day worrying how I was going to tell her Mrs. Schneider wouldn't be coming back and that was her reaction." He rolled his eyes. "Children."

"Well," Anne said, "what was your answer? Can she have a puppy?"

"Do I have a choice?" He raised his voice and looked directly at his daughter in order to get her attention. "She's even promised she'll get up every morning to take it for a walk."

"And feed it, too?" Anne asked.

"Naturally." Ben laughed. "Doesn't every child feed her pet?" He pulled out a chair from the kitchen table and sat down, his eyes lovingly following Rosalind. "Can we strike a deal for one of the pups?"

"Oh, I couldn't possibly sell one." Anne could see Rosalind's head turn sharply. Anne paused a moment. "But I would be pleased to give Rosalind whichever one she chooses."

"That's too generous," Ben protested. "Those dogs are pedigreed and I know they're expensive. I insist on paying you."

"Well, I guess Rosie will just have to do without one then, because it's either a gift or no dog."

Rosalind dashed across the room, her eyes full of entreaty. Debbie lay nestled in her arms. Ben looked at his daughter and then at Anne. "Women! You two are ganging up on me. Okay, I'll agree, but only if you'll have dinner with us tonight. And tomorrow."

"And the next day," Rosalind added for good measure.

Anne smiled in agreement. It was so easy being with father and daughter—so comfortable. Why then, she wondered, did she fell so ill at ease when Rosalind wasn't around?

Even though Ben had given her more responsibility at work and she felt satisfied and secure about her job, whenever he entered her office, her palms became moist and her pulse accelerated. His unapproachable demeanor still made her nervous, but when the two of them were alone socially, it was even worse. With Rosalind around, she could relax and talk to him. Of course, then the subject usually involved children or animals or the weather.

Why were her emotions so at odds? Maybe it had something to do with her inexperience. She'd probably be more comfortable at work in a few months; after all, it was getting easier each day. But what if she was alone with him—on a date? *That's nothing to worry about,* she told herself finally, *because it's never going to happen.*

"HI, WHERE'S ROSIE?" Anne asked, trying not to sound anxious.

It was Monday night. Ben, Anne and Rosalind had been together for the past two days. After the movie on Saturday, they'd had dinner, and on Sunday they fed the ducks at Town Lake, followed by fried chicken and macaroni and cheese at Anne's house. Tonight they were to eat out again.

They'd agreed on a casual meal at a hamburger place, but Ben's attire wasn't casual at all. He was dressed in an expensive sport coat and slacks, which made Anne glad she'd put on a skirt and sweater instead of the jeans she'd originally planned to wear.

"Billie's with her. I decided we needed an adult evening for a change." Ben's eyes met Anne's. "Please don't argue."

"But I hate dragging you away from Rosalind. You didn't need to feel obligated to go out tonight."

"I wanted to be obligated, Anne."

They went to a small French restaurant that had recently opened. "A bit more upscale than hamburgers," Anne said as Ben ordered a bottle of wine. She felt her palms dampen. This was just like a real date—how did a woman act on a date when she hadn't had one in almost two decades?

The brief pairings Tyler had arranged hardly counted. There had only been a few of them and none of those men had made her feel the way Bennett Weston did—restless and unsettled. She didn't want to care about him. Her new life was just falling into place. She didn't want to complicate everything by getting romantically involved with a man—especially this man.

"You look like you're headed for the gallows. Are a few hours alone with me that unpalatable?" Ben had lifted his glass of wine in a toast, but now he was frowning.

Anne raised her glass to his. "Of course not. This is just . . . different."

"Is that good or bad?"

"I'm not sure—it's been a long time."

"You mean no relationships since your husband?"

She shook her head. "Not really."

"Well then, it *has* been a long time."

"Yes. Yet in some ways . . . it's like it was just yesterday. Some mornings when I wake up I don't know where all those years went."

"I know. I feel the same way. I'll soon be forty—where did the last decade go? We have a lot in common, Anne." Ben's gaze had that seductive glow again. He was looking at her the way a man looks at a woman he cares for. Anne wondered how she could ever have thought him cold. Ben's eyes were almost smoldering now.

He changed the subject to something more innocuous and less personal. He seemed to be making a conscious effort to help her relax. They talked about books—Ben liked nonfiction and mysteries, and since he'd recently read a new book, he was eager to tell her about it.

"It's about the removal of the Cherokees from the South into Indian Territory—the area that's now the state of Oklahoma. The Indians didn't want to leave their homes so they decided to fight President Jackson through the courts. And they won. The Supreme Court ruled in their favor. But Jackson said, 'Justice Marshall made the decision, let him enforce it,' and sent the Cherokees on their way. Their migration has been known as the Trail of Tears ever since."

"Sounds like a good book, something I might really like. My mother's family came from Oklahoma. My grandfather was a Chickasaw."

Ben reached across the table and fingered a strand of her blond hair. "Yes, I can definitely see the Indian heritage." He smiled.

The teasing gesture disconcerted Anne. She was more at ease with the impersonal. "So... what else have you read?"

She was relieved to be talking books again. She liked poetry; he mentioned Tom Clancy's latest novel.

"I enjoy mysteries, too," she continued. "And, like most women, I enjoy a little romance—"

"Men like a little romance, too," he interrupted.

"I'm talking about books."

"Of course."

"I guess you wouldn't call me a bookworm, but I like to carry a paperback around with me, for whenever I have to wait. It's also a lot easier to read a paperback in bed."

"Seems a shame—someone as beautiful as you spending all that time in bed reading."

Tonight Ben seemed to have a one-track mind. He was as determined to keep the conversation personal as she was to keep it light. And he seemed to be winning the match. She glanced at her watch. "Don't you think we'd better be going?"

"If you say so." He signaled the waiter.

BEN FOLLOWED HER through the back door and trailed behind her as she flipped on switches to light the darkened house. "Would you like some coffee?" she said.

"Sure."

They went back to the kitchen. Anne pulled out the coffee canister and spooned grounds into the filter-lined basket.

"Are you sure about the dog?" Ben asked. He'd squatted beside Ginger's box, picking up and inspecting one little animal after another. Now he was eyeing Debbie. "I think Rosalind put you on the spot."

"I'm not the only one she put on the spot." Anne laughed. "What about you? Do you honestly think you could've talked her out of that puppy?"

"No," Ben answered. He put Debbie down and moved to the sink to wash his hands.

Anne was standing against the counter watching the coffee drip into the clear glass carafe. Ben came up to her, placing his hands on the counter on either side of her, effectively trapping her. His body leaned into hers; she could feel his breath in her hair. Her head went up and she turned around to face him. "Ben—"

The words were caught in her mouth as it met his. The kiss was long and soft and warm. The kind of kiss Anne hadn't experienced since... She pushed her hands against Ben to break the contact. "Please don't."

"But I want to—and you want to."

"You have no idea what I want." She ducked under his arms to escape him. Confronting him from a safer distance, she said, "Not long ago you thought I was having an affair with Tyler. Now you're coming on to me as if you'd like the affair to be with you."

"So?" He crossed his arms and lounged against the cabinet.

"So maybe we don't want the same things," she said.

"I want to get to know you better, to hold you in my arms."

"To take me to bed."

"Eventually," Ben admitted. "But not until you're ready. I only kissed you, Anne."

"That's no big deal, I suppose. Well, maybe not for you, but for me..." She stopped herself. How could she explain how she felt?

He'd probably think it strange if he knew she'd had no lover since David. It was doubtful he'd correctly interpreted her admission of no serious relationships to mean celibacy—especially after earlier labeling her the femme fatale of Austin. Anne didn't want to clarify matters, either. She didn't want to feel that exposed in front of Ben.

"Please go."

"I'm not going to apologize for kissing you."

"I didn't ask you to apologize. I asked you to leave."

"Without my coffee?"

"Grab a cup at some fast food place."

Ben smiled, as though he might be enjoying her distress. "Okay, I suppose you need your beauty sleep. I don't want you grumpy tomorrow. Dinner again?"

"I'm busy."

"But Rosalind will be disappointed."

"Quit trying to blackmail me through your daughter. I said no. I'm not going out with you again."

"You're a coward, Anne Marshall."

ANNE STARED into the bathroom mirror as she brushed her teeth. Was that the face of a coward? Of course not. The reflection was simply a person who wasn't ready for involvement—not yet. It was simply a matter of too much too soon. The boys had just left. She needed to learn how to fly solo before taking on a copilot.

CHAPTER SEVEN

BEN CALLED ON SATURDAY with an invitation for dinner. Anne refused. Despite the intense attraction she felt for him, she held back in an effort to pace herself. This relationship was heating up too rapidly. For years, her life had moved along slowly—the waiting, the grief, the long adjustment to widowhood. It was too soon for this roller-coaster ride.

On Sunday Ben came by with Rosalind in tow, ostensibly to see Debbie. Again he dropped in without calling first, as though he knew she would have put him off with some excuse if he had. The Westons tried to get Anne to join them for hamburgers, but she declined. "I'm sorry, I've already made plans for the evening."

While Rosalind returned the pup to its mother, Ben edged closer to Anne. "Still running scared?" he whispered.

"Not at all. But I'm convinced we should get our relationship back on a professional basis."

"Don't you think it's already progressed too far for that?"

"Then it'll just have to unprogress."

He looked as though he wanted to pursue the subject further, but Rosalind had turned and was watching them, so he said nothing more.

When they'd left, Anne again felt that unfamiliar depression. Not that she'd never been depressed before; she had, but this was different. She didn't know what was happening to her. Perhaps she needed to get out of the house—see a movie, go shopping—anything to get her mind off Ben and Rosalind.

The movie and window-shopping trip didn't help. Hours later Anne lay in bed trying to concentrate on a new paperback, but her mind remained on Ben. After reading several pages without comprehension, she set the novel aside and switched out the light, only to remain awake for hours, lost in thought.

Why was Ben rushing her into a relationship? With his history, what little she knew of it anyway, she'd have expected him to be as wary of involvement as she was. Why had the man, almost hostile to her at first, suddenly become an ardent admirer? What had caused such a dramatic change? Anne replayed all their recent encounters in her mind. Her nocturnal analyzing kept coming back to Rosalind. Was she the reason for his determined pursuit? Rosalind liked being around Anne. Did Ben think a romantic relationship was necessary to ensure her presence in the child's life?

Not that it mattered, she decided, strengthening her resolve not to get any further involved. Her heart was on the mend, and she had a notion Ben Weston might be the man to break it all over again. She could care about Ben—really care—and there was danger in caring. She wasn't ready to face that danger just yet.

"I THOUGHT HANNAH was cooking dinner," Jody teased. He picked up the last of the four pies Anne had baked and carried them out to the station wagon. A chocolate cake and a plate of pralines were already there.

"Anything else, Mom?" James grabbed a basketball from the closet. "Can we take one of the pups to show Granddad? Pretty soon they'll be big enough to leave Ginger."

"No, he's seen the litter. They'll be around here for a while if he wants to see them again. I think they should be at least eight weeks old before we adopt them out."

"Just the right age for Christmas presents," Jody said as he came back into the house.

The drive out to Tyler's was pleasant. The boys kept the conversation going, teasing her about driving too slowly and about her white-knuckled grip on the steering wheel. "I'm so glad you two came home to keep me humble," she said.

"It's a dirty job," Jody answered, "but somebody's got to do it." He turned to James in the back. "Remember when she ran into the fireplug in front of the house?"

"Please, not that story again," Anne begged, but the two were off and running and kept it up until they drove into the private road leading to Tyler's large ranch house.

"Whose Porsche is that?" James asked.

Craning to see, Anne felt a jolt of anxiety. Or was it excitement? It was definitely a feeling that was becoming increasingly familiar. She hadn't expected Ben to be there. After all, he and Tyler were merely business acquaintances. And neither man had said a word about Ben's coming. Anne had kept her distance all week and so had Ben. No calls, no more drop-in visits to her home, and at work, he had resumed his aloof restraint.

What were he and Rosie doing here? Ben had told her they had no family. Anne strongly suspected that this was a ploy of Tyler's to encourage her to reconsider her decision.

As she stopped the car, Tyler came outside to welcome them. Anne couldn't say much to her father-in-law because behind him was Rosalind, who immediately ran down the steps to hug Anne. "I've been waiting for you," the little girl squealed.

She then turned to James and Jody, almost as though they were her big brothers. "Do you remember me?" she asked.

"Sure we do," they answered together. She held up her arms, so Jody picked her up and swung her into the air. Both boys cast those familiar questioning looks Anne's way.

Ben hadn't joined the welcoming committee. Instead he remained at the door, leaning against the frame, his pale blue eyes studying Anne, almost challenging her. "Here I am again," the eyes seemed to say. "You're not going to get rid of me easily."

The group went into the house where the smell of roasted turkey and corn-bread dressing wafted through the air. James and Jody's expressions changed from questioning to all-knowing as Anne introduced Ben to them.

After she and the boys had retrieved the desserts from the car, Anne excused herself and slipped off to the kitchen. "I'm sure Hannah can use some help."

But Hannah wasn't about to share her kitchen today. "Anne, honey, you go on back in there with the family. I've got everything under control here." She opened the oven and inspected a huge sweet-potato casserole. A heavenly aroma rose up as she poked the bubbling contents.

Anne didn't want to leave. Ben's presence made her feel uncomfortable and the kitchen was a haven for her tangled emotions. Her mind said she didn't want him in her life, didn't want anyone in her life, but her heart said something else. She'd had the strongest impulse to throw herself into his arms when she'd seen him in the doorway. The sensations he caused were almost alien to her, and her only protection seemed to be to deny their existence. Yet that was becoming more and more difficult.

Reluctantly she returned to the den to find Tyler alone. "Where's the crew?" she asked.

"The boys, all three of them, are outside playing basketball." Tyler had installed a court on his lawn when the twins were young and they still used it. "Rosalind went out with them." Anne crossed the room to watch them through the big floor-to-ceiling window. The scene looked so right—so . . . familylike. Anne's reverie was interrupted by Tyler's next words. "I hope you're not angry with me, Anne."

"For interfering?" Her voice sounded sharper than she'd intended. She knew Tyler only wanted what was best for her, but his decisions were based on what *he* thought was best, not necessarily on what really was.

"Ben is very fond of you," Tyler said. "Don't you think you ought to give him a chance?"

Anne turned from the window to face him. "Did he run to you for help?"

"Of course not. He's not that kind of man. I just put two and two together."

"For a lot of reasons, I'm not ready for a relationship," Anne said. She came over to sit on the couch beside Tyler and placed a hand on his arm. "Ben's a fine person but the timing is wrong. Please accept that and stop your matchmaking efforts."

"Anne, I *did* mean well. I know how much you loved David, but lately I've begun to really worry about you. My dear, it's time to move on. When my first wife died in childbirth, I was totally distraught. She had been the love of my youth, such a beauty... I felt so guilty, so shattered. Even more so when the baby died two days later."

Anne was surprised. Despite all the time they'd spent together, Tyler had never spoken to her this way before. Even after Eva's death, he had comforted Anne and the boys without sharing his own pain.

Now his face showed traces of the anguish he must have felt all those years ago when his first wife died. Then there had been the grief at losing Eva after her long battle with multiple sclerosis. And he'd lost two children—first, his baby, then David—a son Tyler couldn't have cherished more if he'd actually fathered him.

Tyler had always been so empathetic, so attuned to her emotions, because he'd suffered great losses, too. She had never really appreciated all the pain this loving man had endured. "I'm sorry," she whispered.

"It was a lifetime ago." He moved to the bar and opened a bottle of wine, pouring a sample, then tasting it, before filling a glass for Anne. "I didn't think I'd ever love again after Marjorie, then I met Eva. If anything, I loved her more. She was the love of my maturity. It was with her that I learned to appreciate the full value of having someone to share my life. And even though it ended in pain, I would never have given up the years we had together.

"Don't cheat yourself out of love, Anne. Believe me, if I found another woman I could care about, I wouldn't hesitate to take a third wife. I'd put the thought of loss behind me and cherish whatever happiness there might be. Life's too short, too fragile, to live any other way. So I keep on the lookout. You should, too." He smiled, softening the seriousness of his earlier words.

Anne felt almost compelled to argue with him, to tell him that it was different for her. But how could she? Tyler had suffered greater loss than she. How could her pain have been any more intense than his? She wouldn't insult him by suggesting that it had.

THE DAY TURNED OUT to be the nicest Thanksgiving in years—for everyone but Anne. Family holidays had always held a trace of loneliness, especially after Eva's death. This one proved to be anything but lonely—instead of the usual family group, there were nine. Besides the Westons, Tyler had included Billie, and Red Fuller and his wife, Frances, for dinner.

The latter three arrived shortly before Hannah started serving the meal. The conversation buzzed and Anne heard Rosalind state her usual "like a real family."

Although Rosalind had said it before, Anne's heart skipped a beat when she heard her. Later she felt another pang when the little girl asked if she could call Tyler Granddad the way the twins did. This time Ben admonished the child not to suggest such familiarities, only to be overruled by Tyler, who told Rosalind he was flattered she wanted to call him Granddad, and that she certainly could.

Tyler was seated at one end of the long table, Anne at the other with Ben on her right. She could hardly ignore him, even if she wanted to. Once, her knee accidentally touched his leg and Anne almost upset her wineglass in her haste to correct the situation.

"Excuse me," she muttered, moving her legs to the other side, this time bumping against Billie's. "Excuse me," she offered again. But Billie hardly noticed; she was too involved in a conversation with Frances Fuller about camellias. Apparently both women were avid gardeners, and were especially fond of the large showy plants, which blossomed in the South during the winter.

"Did I spoil your day by coming?" Ben whispered to her.

"Of course not," she whispered back. "Everyone's pleased that you're here."

"But it's making you very uncomfortable. Why is that?"

She wanted to deny it, but what could she say? It seemed as though Ben was able to see right through her pretense of serenity.

She solved her problem by ignoring him and instead joined in the garden talk with the other women, leaving Ben to speculate with Red about the outcome of the football game.

The meal itself was a feast—a succulent oven-bronzed turkey, rich brown giblet gravy, corn-bread dressing, a sweet-potato casserole oozing with marsh-mallows, an ambrosia of pineapple, mandarin oranges and shredded coconut, green peas and yeasty home-made bread. And just when they all declared they couldn't eat another mouthful, Hannah brought in a cart laden with Anne's desserts.

"Well, if I die of gluttony today," Red joked, "at least I'll go with a smile on my face. Now let me try some of that great-looking pecan pie."

After the meal, they carried their coffee into the den to talk and wait for the football game to start. James and Jody went out to play a little basketball, followed by their four-year-old shadow. Tyler was propped up in his big leather lounge chair. Red and his wife sat on one sofa, and Billie relaxed in the armchair, which left the remaining sofa for Anne and Ben. She was so acutely aware of him she could almost feel her skin prickle.

It was dark when the group finally dispersed. First Red and Frances and Billie left. Then the two Westons. Rosalind spread kisses all around, while Ben shook hands with the boys and Tyler and kissed Anne on the cheek. It was nothing more than a social kiss, certainly nothing passionate, yet Anne felt as though the kiss had been intended for everyone to see. She was still standing on the steps staring after him when his car disappeared around the bend.

"Well, it's late, so don't you think we'd better get a move on, Mumsey?" James had put his arm around her and was steering her inside for final goodbyes. "Jody's got a date."

"And you're going to stay home and keep me company?"

Her son had a chagrined look on his face—a look that told her he had plans, too. Then the expression turned into a devious grin. "But I suspect there's someone around who'd like to keep you company."

"Don't be silly," she said, immediately regretting her sharp tone and hurrying into the house before he could say more.

First Tyler, now her sons. Everyone seemed to be a matchmaker these days. All the way home the twins told her "what a hell of a nice guy Ben is." Anne voiced annoyance at the use of profanity.

"Is that what you're learning at school?"

"Cursing 101," Jody jokingly confirmed. "Quit trying to change the subject, Mom. He *is* a nice guy."

"Sure he is," Anne agreed, "and my boss, remember?"

"I don't think he had work on his mind today," James said.

"Of course not," Anne said evenly. "It's Thanksgiving."

"Yeah, he looked pretty thankful for you," Jody teased.

Anne started to respond with a snappy comeback, but what was the use? The more she protested, the worse they'd get. Tyler was bad enough, but now James and Jody seemed to be reading more into this relationship with Ben than they should. The best thing to do was ignore them.

Ignoring eighteen-year-olds was easier said than done, Anne found. All weekend long they made comments about her not having to stay at home on their account. They even offered to baby-sit Rosalind if she and Ben wanted to go out. Their teasing and curiosity were heightened by the arrival of a dozen yellow roses on Friday morning. They spent the next day singing their own rowdy version of "The Yellow Rose of Texas."

She didn't call to thank Ben for the flowers; instead, she penned a short polite note. Despite the interference of her well-meaning family, she was determined to put her relationship with Ben back in perspective.

He phoned on Saturday, asking her to have dinner. She declined. He suggested Sunday, after the twins had left. She told him she'd already made plans. "Like hell you have," he barked and slammed down the phone. Anne didn't know whether to be hurt or relieved.

ANNE WAS SURPRISED at her reaction to the boys' departure. She had expected to be tearful, which was what had happened the first few times they'd returned home. Instead she felt a strange sort of serenity. Her sons were happy with school, and she was beginning to come to terms with her own life now.

She'd grown used to not waiting up for them to return after a night out with their friends, and to having the house to herself. Although she still missed her sons—they were never far from her mind—there were definitely a few advantages to their absence. One of them, at the moment, was not having to field their questions about Ben and Rosalind.

She had often wondered what the twins would think if she should decide to remarry—but those musings had been vague "what if" questions. If she'd ever had any doubts about whether they would accept someone new in their lives, those doubts were now laid to rest. What with the teasing, the constant references to "Uncle Ben" and the prodding to become more involved with him, James and Jody seemed almost anxious for her to have a relationship.

Had she cheated them these past years? Had they longed for a father? She couldn't help wondering how Ben would fit that image. His only experience with children was with a preschooler. Yet he was a few years older than she was, certainly old enough to have fathered grown sons.

"Why conjecture about something I'm really not interested in?" she asked Ginger, her canine sounding board. "Just like a mother, isn't it? Always feeling guilty about something." She bent down to pet the dog and her nursing puppies. Ginger was an indulgent mother—the puppies were ready to be weaned, yet she made few moves to push them away.

Despite her denials, Anne found it difficult not to focus on Ben and she spent entirely too many hours thinking about him. "I'll take a continuing-education course after the holidays—brush up on my Spanish. Any educated person should know more than one language."

Especially in Texas, she thought, one should know Spanish. It was part of the state heritage, after all. Her conversation with herself was a mixture of speaking aloud and considering what she should do. The discussion took her mind off Ben—at least until the moment she pulled into the parking lot on Monday morning. The only available space was next to his car. Just seeing his Porsche brought him back into her thoughts.

"MAKE A COUPLE of airline reservations for tomorrow morning." Ben was at Billie's desk, a notepad in his hand. They both glanced up as Anne came in. "I need to see you," Ben said, gesturing for her to follow him into his office.

He poured them each a cup of coffee and sat down in the executive chair behind his desk. "We've got a problem and I need your help."

Anne somehow hadn't expected this conversation to be about work. She relaxed a little, but noticed that Ben seemed quite tense. Even though she was always surprised by the difference in the way he behaved at the office and outside it, especially with Rosalind, today there was a noticeable tautness about him.

"Do you remember the file on Tony Seguin?" he said.

Anne nodded.

"Tony helped my career a lot in the early days. The Seguins own a big ranch near Corpus Christi and they want a new ranch house—something spectacular. But Tony and his wife, Carmen, are arguing like cats and dogs about the design. And my involvement doesn't help. Carmen says she won't have two males ramming something down her throat. I probably should have spent more time in her kitchen and less out fishing with Tony. Maybe then she'd trust me more. Anyway, she's insisting on a woman's viewpoint. And you're the only woman I have."

"So what does that mean?" In contrast to her earlier calm on discovering this was to a business conversation, Anne now felt apprehensive. She knew what Ben was going to say next: one of those airline tickets was for her. Had the Seguins really wanted a woman's opinion, or had Ben deftly maneuvered her into spending time with him? Either way, she had little choice but to agree. She could cut him out of her personal life, but she couldn't very well refuse a request from her boss to do something that, at least on the surface, was business-related.

"It means I need you to fly down to Corpus with me. We'll rent a car and drive out to the ranch. Maybe between us, we can get Tony and Carmen to agree on something. They're squabbling so much I'm beginning to wonder if they'll make it to their fortieth wedding anniversary. They just celebrated their thirtieth."

"When do we leave?" If Ben thought she'd try to beg off from this assignment, he was mistaken. She had no intention of letting their other relationship interfere with her professionalism. This was business; she'd treat it that way.

"First thing in the morning. I'll pick you up on my way to the airport, then you won't have to worry about leaving your car there. Plan to stay at least one night, maybe two."

Again she'd anticipated that, had already assumed he planned an overnight trip. Well, that was okay—she had a couple of girlhood friends in Corpus. She could visit with them during the evening and leave Mr. Bennett Weston to his own devices.

"I DON'T WANT another ranch house like this one." Carmen paced up and down the den as she talked, occasionally throwing in a word or two of Spanish. "I want something softer—*muy romantico.*"

Tony raised his hands in frustration. "That crazy wife of mine wants a Southern plantation house, something that would be out of place here. My friends wouldn't feel comfortable. Damn, *I* wouldn't feel comfortable! I'd feel like I needed to import cypress trees and serve mint juleps. No way. We just won't build anything."

Anne had wondered if Ben's rationale that Tony and Carmen couldn't agree was simply an excuse to maneuver her into accompanying him. Now she saw that he really did need a buffer.

They'd arrived at the Seguin ranch before noon, and all through lunch and for several hours afterward, Tony and Carmen had argued about the house. Ben had been patient with his friends, but now he was rubbing the back of his neck in exasperation. He had offered a Spanish-style design that fit the surrounding land perfectly, but both husband and wife had objected. Anne suspected they didn't want to agree on anything at this point.

"Maybe we could take this from the beginning," Anne suggested. "Since I wasn't here, I'm not sure I understand everything. Tony, what do you really want out of a new house?"

"Something I feel at home with, something comfortable."

"Something with antlers on the walls," his wife interjected. It made Anne think of Tyler's home and the mounted deer heads in his den. She couldn't help but share Carmen's distaste for that type of macho surroundings, no matter how luxurious.

"Let me hear from Tony first," Anne warned, treating Carmen almost the way she would one of the twins. Surprisingly, the woman acquiesced.

"And what else do you want?" Anne prodded the man.

"That's all, that's it. Just a homey place I can relax in." He crossed his arms in front of his chest defiantly.

"Is it really? Don't you also want to make Carmen happy? Isn't that your primary purpose in building a new house?" She gestured around the room. "This is a perfectly nice place. So as long as you're going to all the trouble and expense of replacing it, don't you want the new one to please her?"

Tony nodded reluctantly. "But not if I hate it."

"Of course not," Anne soothed. She turned to Carmen. "Now, Carmen, what do you want in a new house? What's most important?"

"I want it to be romantic, *que sea especial. Y con una cocina muy grande.*"

Anne had understood enough of Carmen's Spanish to realize she wanted a big kitchen. She glanced at Ben. His eyes shot to the ceiling and she had to agree with him. These two, with their incompatible ideas, were practically impossible. But they were important to Ben; otherwise, she knew, he would have rolled up his drawings and headed for the door. Anne picked up one of the sketches and spread it across the coffee table. "Have either of you been to Spain?"

They shook their heads.

"You should take Carmen there, Tony. Nothing is more romantic than Seville." Anne was intrigued by Spanish architecture, and had taken a course specifically about the residences of Seville. "Most of the homes have gorgeous inner patios—little gardens. We could tuck away a couple of those gardens in the house. Maybe one near the kitchen, another off the main salon and then perhaps a very private, *muy romantico* little patio by the master bedroom." Anne took a blank sheet of paper and sketched a design showing flowers and a fountain.

Carmen watched closely and silently reached for the drawing when Anne was finished. She cocked her head from side to side, then nodded. She handed the drawing to her husband. He too spent a few moments studying the page, before giving it to Ben and extending his hand. Less than an hour later, Ben and Anne were in their rented car, leaving the Seguin ranch.

Ben grinned at her, shaking his head in mock amazement. "You deserve the best dinner in South Texas for that display of diplomacy and finesse. I was almost ready to call it quits."

"They *are* quite a pair," Anne agreed.

"One of the few happy marriages I've seen," Ben said, then laughed. "I think part of their joy is that they disagree about everything. Maybe it's the kiss-and-make-up aspect that appeals to them." He pulled out from the ranch road onto the highway.

"I know it's been a trying day," Anne said, "but you turned the wrong way."

"No, I didn't. We're going to have a little R and R—rest and relaxation—after that ordeal. Thought we'd spend the night at La Gaviota, Tyler's resort. Have you been there?"

So much for escaping Ben, Anne thought. Now she worried not only about having to deal with her feelings for him, but also about revisiting La Gaviota....

"THERE'S A HEATED POOL if you want to swim, or if you prefer we can just do some beachcombing," Ben told her. The bellman had taken their bags directly upstairs rather than stopping at the registration desk. "Part of the deal with Tyler," Ben said, explaining that he kept a suite at the luxurious hotel.

Her bags were placed in one bedroom, his in the other. Separating the two rooms was a spacious lounge with a private balcony overlooking the Gulf of Mexico. Fresh flowers and a bowl of fruit sat on the coffee table.

Anne wasn't sure what she wanted to do, except avoid being alone with him. It was a pleasant December afternoon, the temperature in the high seventies. A swim sounded appealing. It would soothe taut muscles and help her relax, but unfortunately, she hadn't brought a swimsuit—hadn't even considered packing one. She did have a pair of sweats and her running shoes, though. "Perhaps a walk," she suggested.

They strolled slowly along the sand, neither of them talking, stopping every now and then to inspect something beneath their feet. When Ben took her hand, it seemed so natural that she didn't object. They just kept on walking; Anne was lost in her own thoughts and obviously Ben was just as preoccupied.

They came to some grassy sand dunes. She glanced up at him questioningly and Ben motioned her to sit down. She did, and he joined her, sitting cross-legged on the ground. Together they watched a sand crab skittering nearby. The seashore was always so rejuvenating, so peaceful. For the first time, she felt truly relaxed with Ben.

Finally he broke the silence. "I've wanted to talk to you."

Anne's impulse was to interrupt and say, "Don't spoil it." But she knew there were words unspoken between the two of them, words that had to be said.

Ben poked a stick in the sand as he talked. "I know I've given you a lot of conflicting signals since we met. But I don't have too much experience with loving relationships. The truth is you've become important to me. Very important. I want you to be my wife.''

Anne's pulse accelerated; she hadn't expected a proposal, had no idea how to respond. ''Ben...''

He placed his fingertips on her lips to hush her as though he knew she was going to argue. ''Don't say anything. First you need to understand me—to understand why I'm the way I am. Then maybe...'' He looked into her eyes. ''Remember when we talked about Charlotte—my wife?''

''You told me very little,'' she said. ''I know your marriage wasn't made in heaven, but that's about all.''

''Definitely not heaven. If anything, more like hell.'' He traced a star pattern in the sand. ''For a long time, I've tried not to think about her, to put her totally out of my mind. Most of the time, I succeed. When I don't, some pretty negative thoughts start to emerge.

''I haven't had a lot of success with women in my life. My mother ran off when I was a baby. I never saw her again. Perhaps I can understand her leaving my father—he was a cold unfeeling man, determined to run the lives of everyone around him. Billie was his secretary. How she put up with him, I'll never know, but it's a good thing she did because Billie's the only woman who was ever there for me. The only one who offered me affection and caring while I was growing up.''

Anne now understood Ben's devotion to his secretary. She had suspected they had a history; Billie had revealed as much. His feelings about women in general were also more understandable. He wasn't just coping with his reactions to a bad marriage, but also to the rejection by his mother. He'd said he could understand her leaving his father, but Anne suspected Ben had never accepted her leaving him, too.

"Billie was great, but she couldn't fill every void—I needed more, yet I avoided relationships. When Charlotte finally came along I suppose I was 'ripe for the picking' as the expression goes. She was in her early twenties and I was over thirty but Charlotte pulled the strings. I fell head over heels in love, carried a torch like a schoolboy. My father objected, saying she was only interested in our money, and he was determined she wouldn't get a penny of it. His opposition doubled my resolve to make Charlotte my wife. For once I was going to do something my way." Ben picked up a couple of stones and tossed them into the water.

"I think it galled me as much as anything that she proved him right. When Charlotte became pregnant with Rosalind she was furious. Nothing was working out as she'd planned. Instead of a life of luxury, she was chained to a struggling architect. And she was going to become a mother, the last thing in the world she wanted.

"She tried to blackmail me—and my father—with the baby. Threatened an abortion. Charlotte gave me an ultimatum—either come up with a hundred thousand dollars or she'd end the pregnancy. I panicked. I wanted that baby. I begged my father to help me, told him I'd pay back every penny. He refused."

"Oh, no. What did you do?"

"I'd recently met Tyler Cunningham. One night over a bottle of bourbon, we talked. Actually, he listened while I poured my heart out to him. Then without a word, he got out his checkbook and started writing. Can you believe it? My own father said no, but Tyler—a near stranger—handed over the money without blinking an eye. He lent me the whole amount.''

So that was the reason Ben felt so indebted to Tyler. Now Anne understood. She thought about the timing. Rosalind was four, so this had happened almost five years ago. Probably right after David's body was returned and Eva's health had taken a sudden decline. A time when Tyler himself was feeling alone and vulnerable. He was such a caring man that it wasn't surprising he'd tried to ease Ben's pain.

''What happened to Charlotte?''

''After Rosalind's birth, she took the money and ran.'' Ben threw a few more stones, watching them disappear into the surf. ''She was killed in a car accident about six months later. I suppose it's ironic that my father died a few months after that and I inherited everything that was so important to Charlotte.''

Anne reached over and took his hand. Ben had only given her a bare outline, but it was enough. She didn't need to know any more. The closed look on his face told her he was reliving the torment of those years. She wished she could give him respite from the pain.

CHAPTER EIGHT

HOLDING HANDS, THEY walked back up the beach toward the hotel. In their silence, they communicated more intimately than ever before. Unless she immediately took steps to prevent it, Anne knew what was going to happen. When they returned to the hotel, Ben would take her in his arms...he would kiss her...she would welcome the kiss and then...

Since their first meeting, she had known it would come to this. Had Ben known, too? Was that the reason for his antagonism toward her? Had he been fighting the attraction just as she had? Regardless, Anne had no intention of stopping what was meant to be. Marriage? She couldn't think about that now. Not when she was seized by this sweet torment that wouldn't be assuaged until she was in his arms. No, she could think no further than that. Today somehow existed outside of time—a moment of fleeting magic. She'd had so few in her love life. She wanted to savor it during its brief existence.

They entered the luxurious suite and Ben embraced her just as she'd imagined. His lips were tender, coaxing. His hands stroked her body, moving under her T-shirt to touch bare skin. When he broke the kiss, she was shocked by the sudden sense of loss, her blue eyes searching his, questioning.

Ben picked her up in his arms and carried her to his bedroom, placing her gently across the chocolate-brown satin spread. She watched as he unfastened the buttons of his shirt, revealing the dark hair feathering his muscular chest. Anne's heart beat a staccato rhythm as Ben cast the shirt aside and joined her on the bed. He caressed her cheek with the back of his hand, then, as if in slow motion, he lowered his head to seal his lips on hers. Her breath quickened along with his. Overwhelmed by emotion, she couldn't prevent the escape of a solitary tear, its dampness marking a trail down her temple.

Ben kissed the tear away. "What's wrong, love?"

The endearment caught her by surprise. Somehow she hadn't thought of Ben as a man who whispered tender words. If anything his gentleness only confused her more. "It's been such a long time," she said. "What if...?"

"There's been no one since...?"

He left off the rest of the sentence but Anne knew what he was asking. She gave her head a slow negative shake, "I'm—"

He hushed her with another kiss. "Don't be. Don't be afraid, love."

"I've probably forgotten what to do."

He laughed gently. "I understand it's just like riding a bicycle."

"The last time I rode a bicycle I fell off and broke my arm."

"I won't hurt you, Anne." His fingers entwined in the silky curls of her blond hair. "I promise I won't hurt you."

Responding to the sincerity in his voice, she couldn't help but believe him and be comforted. The next hours were spent exploring each other's bodies, each other's reactions. The first time was sweet and gentle, the second heated and passionate, the third a combination of fire and tenderness.... Anne hadn't envisioned an entire afternoon of passion, and yet she'd been an equal participant. They'd talked little—it was as though each was afraid that conversation would somehow break the spell.

"Tired?" Ben's head was propped up on one hand and he stroked Anne's brow with the fingertips of the other.

"A little. Mainly hungry. We haven't eaten since noon."

"Worked up an appetite, have you? Well, I'd better get you a little sustenance, woman, because I want you to have plenty of energy for later." He was smiling at her. This was yet another Bennett Weston. That no-nonsense demeanor had been replaced by a teasing lighthearted attitude. Anne found these different facets intriguing. She studied him as he picked up the telephone, surprised that instead of ordering room service, he made dinner reservations.

He replaced the receiver and turned to her, answering her unspoken question. "Another place, and wild horses couldn't drag me from the room. Unfortunately Chef Ferdinand knows me and always insists on pulling out all the stops for my visits. If I don't appear in the dining room tonight, I've got to come up with a very good explanation. I'd rather not. Do you agree?"

"I agree."

"Don't look so disappointed. I promise you the meal will be worth it—almost." Then he laughed, that soft husky laugh she heard so seldom but was growing to cherish.

"Well..." She rose from the bed, clutching the sheet, and reached for her clothes. "This Ferdinand must be quite a cook."

"Believe me, tonight he'll be my major competition."

They played as they dressed, Ben stealing kisses and caressing her as she tried to apply fresh makeup. It took over an hour for her to finish getting ready. Then they went downstairs to the dining room, which was located at the end of a pier, jutting out onto the water. Huge windows provided a dramatic ocean view.

Ben ordered oysters on the half shell as an appetizer. "Insurance," he told her with a smile. Anne knew oysters were supposed to be an aphrodisiac, but judging by what had happened this afternoon, she doubted either of them needed it. Just being together seemed enough.

When he heard that Ben had arrived, Chef Ferdinand came bustling out of the kitchen. He was charming and dictatorial, telling them what they would have tonight: bouillabaisse, shrimp with artichokes, and pasta with dried tomatoes. Dessert would be a surprise. "Oh, and champagne, don't you think?" Ferdinand said.

Ben nodded. "A bottle of Taittinger's."

Anne froze. Suddenly it all seemed wrong. She hadn't given David a single thought until now. Taittinger's had been *their* champagne. She'd been David's wife. Suddenly she felt so disloyal. All those years of waiting and yearning, promising herself that no one would ever take his place, only to fall for a man almost overnight, and in the process, push David into the background.

Ben didn't notice her change of mood, and she tried to hide it from him. It wasn't his fault; he'd had no way of knowing. Still, the gaiety, the spontaneity, had vanished for Anne, replaced by a feeling of uneasiness.

"You're quiet." Ben took her hand. "Have I worn you out?"

Anne gave a weak nod. "I'm not used to..."

"To having someone in your bed?" He smiled. "I'm not either, you know. Although I think I could get used to it rather easily, as long as you were that someone." He turned up the palms of her hands and gave each one a kiss. Anne smiled at the tender gesture, but she felt like Cinderella at the stroke of midnight. The enchantment had vanished.

WHEN THEY RETURNED to the suite, Ben immediately folded her in his arms. Anne was wooden. The connection between them had been broken and she couldn't seem to get it back. If Ben sensed the change, he didn't comment on it. Yet when Anne headed toward her bedroom, he stopped her. "Aren't you going to sleep with me? I want to hold you through the night.''

A part of her protested, but how could she explain a refusal after what they'd shared this afternoon? Besides, she had to admit she wanted to be with him. To sleep with him, to make love with him, to lose herself in his arms, to momentarily forget the past. She would make the most of this night—there might never be another.

Nestled in his arms in the darkened bedroom, Anne began to feel at peace. Ben was massaging her taut muscles, soothing her. He had apparently noticed the difference in her mood, but rather than forcing her to talk about it, he had chosen to simply love her. Giving, not taking...loving unselfishly. His words were gentle calming words of love. ''Your body is so beautiful...I've wanted to hold you like this for so long...I love you, Anne.''

''I love you, too,'' she answered, realizing for the first time that she truly did.

When morning came, they made love again. But this time it was rough and intense, almost hurtful. Ben seemed to be responding to her silent messages, her fears, somehow seemed to know this lovemaking could be their last. Yet, when it was over and they lay side by side giving their spent bodies a chance to return to normal, he said again, ''I do want you to be my wife. I know you may need time to think about marriage, and I'll give it to you. But not too much. We shouldn't waste any more time. We've both wasted enough as it is. We've both waited too long.''

"Ben . . ." She knew she had to tell him how impossible this was, yet she couldn't bring herself to do it. Despite her allegiance to David, maybe a new relationship, a new marriage, was possible, after all.

He turned to face her. "Think about it, love. Don't answer now, just think about it. I'll ask you again in a week. Till then we won't mention it."

"GOOD MORNING," chimed Billie and Lisa as Anne walked into the office the next day.

"Good morning," Anne answered as she breezed through the reception area to her own office.

She settled at her desk, and instead of going through her usual morning ritual—checking her calendar, reading the mail, getting a cup of coffee—she gazed out the window, daydreaming. It was a beautiful December day with a hint of late-autumn crispness in the air. She could see her reflection in the window—the black wool suit softened by an ivory silk blouse. She looked no different, but she felt totally changed.

She straightened the collar of her suit. It was one of her recent going-to-work purchases, but Austin hadn't been cool enough to wear it until today. The city had experienced an unusually warm fall and only now was it beginning to seem like December. For the first time, she felt inclined to start her Christmas shopping. Until now, the weather had been too summery—and she'd had too much on her mind.

Anne thought of the coming Christmas season. The latter half of December had always been difficult for her. She was lonelier than usual then, yet she had to conceal her unhappiness because of the boys. Being the lone Santa Claus and maintaining a familylike atmosphere despite the absence of a father drained her emotionally.

Fortunately Anne's parents made a point of being with the three of them at Christmas. They usually came to Austin in their big recreational vehicle, although once or twice she and the boys had traveled to Arizona. And, of course, there was Tyler. Still, it was a time she had to fight off feelings of aloneness, of depression. More than once, Anne had longed for brothers and sisters, for the boisterousness of a big family.

This year Christmas would be different. Her parents were planning a trip to Texas, and the boys would be coming home. Tyler would be there. But the added dimension was the presence of Ben and Rosalind. It would be fun to see the holidays again through a small child's eyes. And a little girl at that.

Anne considered some new Christmas decorations for the yard, maybe some outside lights for the trees, as well as for the eaves of the house. She'd also dig out her cookbooks and begin filling the freezer with home-baked goods. Christmas was only a few weeks away and she couldn't leave everything until the last minute. She picked up a white memo pad and jotted down a few gift ideas. For the first time in years, she found herself anticipating the holidays instead of dreading them.

ANNE WAS AT HER DRAFTING board sketching ideas for the Seguins' patios when Ben entered her office, followed by Willie and Mason. He moved around behind her, putting his hand on the back of her chair as he explained the plans for the new house to their colleagues. Anne was a little shocked by this unexpectedly possessive gesture.

Except for that kiss early on, it was the first time Ben had been anything but totally professional with her in the office. He seemed to be going out of his way to make their relationship clear to the others—and possibly send a message to Mason. Surprisingly his actions didn't embarrass her. Instead she felt a sense of satisfaction, of belonging, that had been absent from her life for too long.

When the two men left, Ben closed the door behind them. "I have to run down to Houston tomorrow, so I need to spend some time with Rosalind tonight. Will you have dinner with us?"

Anne nodded. "What time?" she asked, happy she could agree. It was Thursday but Tyler was out of town. Their weekly get-together had been postponed until Saturday, when they were meeting for brunch.

Ben moved close enough to put his arms around her. "Six-thirty," he whispered. "Rosalind gets hungry early." He then kissed her—a long, long passionate kiss. "I'm hungry now," he murmured. "Too bad the office is so crowded." He took a white handkerchief from his pocket and wiped the traces of Anne's pink lipstick from his mouth. "See you tonight."

The day went by quickly for Anne. She was engrossed in completing the initial designs they'd discussed. Ben was catching up on phone calls and correspondence he'd missed while they were in Corpus Christi. Several times Billie came into Anne's office, once to ask if she needed any office supplies, then to bring her the mail, and at noon to ask Anne to join her for lunch.

Anne guessed that Billie wanted to talk to her alone, since all recent attempts at a private conversation had been foiled by their coworkers. Lisa had become Billie's constant shadow, something the older woman seemed to appreciate most of the time, and when Lisa wasn't around, one of the men was. Billie's plans, however, were thwarted again when Hank invited himself along for lunch.

Actually Anne was grateful for his presence. She wasn't ready to talk to anyone about her relationship with Ben. Not yet. It was so new, and she was still savoring the wonder of it all. At this point, the romance was too fragile to share.

"WHEN CAN DEBBIE come home with me?" Rosalind was kneeling beside Ginger's basket watching the wriggling pups. Ginger had left the litter and was out in the yard with Fred. The puppies were ready to go to new homes now, but Anne had told the boys they would have one last chance to see them at Christmas. This would be Ginger's last litter. Fred had already been neutered and Ginger would be spayed in a few weeks. Much as Anne loved puppies, she didn't want to be an irresponsible pet owner.

"Very soon," she promised, chasing after one of the straying Labs and returning it to the basket. Rosalind headed in the other direction retrieving another puppy, which scrabbled back out of the basket as fast as its tiny legs could take it.

Ben was leaning against the kitchen cabinet, watching the activity with a look of indulgent humor. "If you two are finished playing with the animals, shall we go to dinner?"

They ate at a small Chinese restaurant near the university. The conversation again centered on Rosalind, but also, this time, on Christmas.

"Know what I've asked Santa to bring me?"

"What's that, Rosie?" Anne asked.

"It's a secret. Only Santa and me know."

"Only Santa and I," Ben corrected.

"But you don't know, Daddy. Just Santa and me."

Ben looked across the table at Anne and shrugged. "Hard to refute that logic." They both laughed.

The little group went back to Anne's house immediately after dinner. Ben and Rosalind saw Anne inside. Then Ben flicked on all the lights and checked to make sure everything was in order before leaving her alone. He suggested they have dinner at his house on Saturday. "About time you came to our place. You've never even seen it."

Anne agreed and walked the two of them to the car. Rosalind skipped ahead as Ben pulled Anne into his arms for a good-night kiss. The kiss lasted long seconds before Anne pushed him away. "Rosalind," she reminded him.

"Rosalind wouldn't object," Ben answered, giving her another quick kiss, then moving to join the child.

He had just opened the car door to help her inside when she ran back to Anne. "Want to know my secret?" she whispered. "What I asked Santa for?"

Anne nodded with a smile, realizing what a compliment it was for Rosalind to share the confidence.

"I asked for a mommy," Rosalind said. She kissed Anne quickly and hurried to the car.

BILLIE CORNERED HER early the next morning, bringing coffee and doughnuts into Anne's office and shutting the door behind her. "I've been wanting to talk to you ever since Thanksgiving. To tell you how it does my heart good to see you with Ben and Rosie."

"They're very special," Anne said softly.

"Ben's almost a different person," Billie continued. "And that precious child—she's like my own granddaughter, you know."

Anne nodded, aware that Billie had never married, that Ben and Rosalind were the closest thing to family she had. "She's a cutie."

"Indeed. And she thinks you hung the moon. If ever I saw a child who wanted a mother, that one does. She's a lucky little girl Ben found you, a woman he can finally trust." Billie came over to hug her. "I just wanted to tell you that."

Anne returned the hug. "Thanks, Billie."

The older woman gave her a warm smile, then picked up her coffee cup and left the office.

Anne moved to her drafting table, intending to continue her work on the Seguins' patios. Somehow she couldn't concentrate. Billie had meant her visit to be supportive and encouraging, but it had been anything but. Anne knew how much Ben loved his daughter, how he'd do anything for her, give her anything he could. If Rosalind had picked Anne for a mother, would he grant that wish, too? Would he put aside his contempt for marriage just to please Rosalind?

As Anne was trying to shake off her doubts, she was dismayed to see Mason enter her office. For the most part, he ignored her now, preferring to flirt with the younger Lisa. But it appeared that Mason was determined to talk to her today.

"So it looks like you've been assigned high-level duties."

"You mean the Seguin project? Well, that's easy to explain—"

"Don't be silly," he said. "Not those bickering Seguins—I'm talking about a much higher calling, namely being anointed new mommy for Rosalind. I have to hand it to Ben—Anne Marshall, experienced mother of twins, homemaker *extraordinaire,* and all-around soft touch—what a perfect choice to fill the gap left by Frau Schneider."

"What are you talking about?" Anne's voice had risen, her pale skin flushed.

"Nothing, nothing. Don't get all upset." He raised his palms toward her. "Just teasing. Can't you take a little joke, Annie?" He turned abruptly and walked out of her office.

Anne sat staring. First Billie, and now Mason. Could they be right? Had Ben's sudden interest in her been intensified by Mrs. Schneider's departure and his subsequent baby-sitting problem? She'd wondered before and hadn't come to any conclusion. But now the notion was more unsettling, even as she tried to deny it. Ben could have given Rosalind a mother long ago, Anne argued, recalling the number of women who phoned him at the office hoping to be the one who got his attention. Everyone at Weston and Associates joked about the calls. Even Lisa had joined in, days after starting her job. "It's another of his girlfriends," she'd announce to Billie or Anne several times a week.

So why me? Anne wondered. Surely it was more than just a four-year-old child's stamp of approval. Ben had indicated that Charlotte had been unfaithful. "A woman he can finally trust." That was what Billie had said. Was her constancy another motivation? A woman who'd been faithful to her husband for a dozen years after his plane was shot down, a woman who'd had no serious involvement since.... A twinge of unrest niggled at Anne.

She wished Ben was here, not in Houston. She needed to be with him, needed his reassurance. Without it, doubts began to seep into her mind and make her question everything that had happened between them. Did Ben want a wife for himself? Or did he want a mother for Rosalind? Making love had been wonderful, more than she could ever have hoped for. Still, sexual compatibility didn't automatically equal love. What was he really after?

While she was wrestling with those questions, another one entered her mind: would Ben expect her to quit work and stay home with Rosie? Anne recalled her uncertainties about entering the work force, but now that she'd settled in, she'd begun to enjoy the business world and she wasn't sure she wanted to be a homemaker again. Although she'd been content with her life, now she enjoyed the satisfaction she got from applying her years of schooling.

Ben probably wouldn't want his wife working for him. Even if he located a temporary nanny for Rosalind, he still needed some permanent arrangement. Mrs. Schneider wasn't planning to return and, as Ben well knew, good child care was difficult to find. A wife and mother was the best answer for any man raising a child alone.

To make use of her nervous energy in Ben's absence, Anne decided to begin her Christmas shopping on the way home from work. But despite the cheery holiday decorations and the enthusiastic faces of other shoppers, Anne found it hard to lose herself in the season. Absentmindedly, she purchased several small gifts for the boys—socks, albums, gag calendars—and a new book about the space program Tyler had mentioned he wanted to read.

She also bought an ounce of her mother's favorite perfume and a bottle of men's cologne for her father. Then she realized she had absolutely no idea what to get for Ben. That thought upset her, and finally she gave up, too preoccupied to do any more shopping. Even the festive Christmas music couldn't lighten her mood. She might as well head home.

Anne followed her typical evening routine, feeding the animals, making herself a light meal, watching a little television. She took a new paperback to bed and tried to get involved in the story. But nothing managed to take her mind off Ben. Why had he really asked her to marry him? Especially this soon. They'd only known each other since September—a short three months. Enough time, perhaps, to fall in love. Not enough time to be sure that what they felt would really last.

"I RAN INTO BEN at the airport. He tells me things are fine between the two of you." Tyler picked up a croissant and broke it apart, spreading blackberry jelly on one piece.

"Yes, everything's going well."

"You don't sound very convincing. What's wrong?"

"Ben's getting serious . . . talking marriage." Tyler had always been her confidant. Now, more than ever, she needed to speak with someone about her ambivalent feelings. "I don't think I'm ready for that yet."

"You don't have to let Ben rush you into anything. Take your time." He reached for the coffee carafe on the table and filled her cup. "Don't wait too long, though. I doubt you'll find a better man, and neither of you is getting any younger."

"Thanks for the reminder—just what a woman nearing forty wants to hear."

"Come on, Anne, you know what I mean. You two aren't juveniles who can't trust their own feelings."

If Tyler meant his remarks to be comforting, he was certainly missing the boat, Anne thought wryly. "It's because we *are* older that there are so many things to consider. For instance, the boys—how would they react?" She sipped the fresh coffee.

"James and Jody are well on the way to leading their own lives. I think they'd want you to be happy. Anyway, they seem to like Ben."

"But it's such a big step."

"Yes, it is." He covered her hand with his. "The safe way isn't always the best way, Anne. I think you and Ben need each other, and Rosalind needs a mother. Who knows, maybe those twins of yours could use a father. This could work out to everyone's advantage. I know I'd be proud to claim Ben as a member of the family."

"Got everything figured out, haven't you?" She eyed him warily.

"Don't give me too much credit. I only call them like I see them. This time it's fate."

"Hmm."

Anne and Tyler parted company in the restaurant parking lot, she on her way to the hairdresser, Tyler to a basketball game. She sat in her car for a couple of moments after he'd driven off. Her conversation with her father-in-law hadn't eased any of her worries. Instead, she was even more certain that what Ben really wanted was a mother for Rosalind. Much as Anne had come to love the little girl, the thought was painful. She needed him to want her for himself—not just for his daughter.

Anne realized she was a product of her generation—the idealistic romantic generation. Women who still dreamed about a knight in shining armor. The two of them living happily ever after. Although she'd learned that life seldom happened that way, that happy-ever-afters were rare indeed, practical common-sense reasons for getting married still weren't for her. So maybe Rosalind *did* need a mother. Maybe the boys *could* use a father. Maybe she *needed* a husband

and maybe Ben *needed* a wife. But to her, none of these reasons seemed enough for marriage.

She and David had been head over heels in love. And if she ever married again, she wanted to feel those same emotions. Otherwise her first marriage would, inevitably, overshadow the second.

AFTER LEAVING the hairdresser's, Anne made a series of mundane stops—picking up the dry cleaning, shopping for groceries, filling the car with gas. She also visited the hardware store and purchased a few sets of miniature outdoor Christmas lights for the trees.

Her mind wasn't on those tasks; instead, she was assessing her life—how it was now, how it might have been had David lived. They would have soon been celebrating their twentieth anniversary. And with the twins in college, they'd have had more time for each other. Or would they have? Would there have been other children? Probably. David had loved children and had often expressed his desire for a large family. Anne had wanted that, too.

But what did she want now? Ben would probably repeat his marriage proposal tonight. And this time he'd expect an answer. He'd called the night before, after getting home from Houston. It had been close to midnight and he'd apologized for phoning so late, saying he hoped he hadn't awakened her. He'd had to hear her voice, he'd said. Anne was in bed, but she wasn't asleep. She'd been half-reading, half-dozing, hoping to hear from him. The call caused her heart to flutter. It was surprising how quickly the courtship routine—and her reactions to it—had become familiar.

Ben went on to discuss the difficulty of waking Rosalind so they could drive the sitter home. Normally the woman would have used her own car, but it had been so late he didn't want her out alone.

It was a casual conversation, yet Anne couldn't ignore the implication that if he and Anne were married there would be no need to disturb Rosalind. Another reminder of Anne's value as a surrogate mother. After the call, she remained wide awake, filled with renewed misgivings about their relationship.

Anne spent the afternoon making a three-layer chocolate cake to take to Ben's for dessert. They'd already agreed that she would drive over; his house was only two or three miles from hers. The fact that she had yet to see it simply reinforced how short a time they'd known each other.

CHAPTER NINE

ANNE DROVE THROUGH THE hilly residential streets and into Ben's neighborhood. The homes were an eclectic mixture, ranging from stark modern to colonial. Beyond the backyards with their terraces and blue swimming pools were the hills that flanked the west side of Austin. She turned into a short side street and saw the familiar Porsche parked in the circular drive of the last house on the block.

Ben's house was one of the more modern homes in the area, all brick and wood and glass. The yard was landscaped with ground covers, rather than the conventional manicured grass. Plants and rocks were interspersed with trees.

The front door swung open the minute she pulled into the drive, as though Ben had been watching for her. More than likely, it was Rosalind watching she thought, and announcing Anne's arrival.

"Hello, love." He greeted her with a kiss.

"The neighbors," Anne protested.

Ben laughed. "I do believe my future wife is a tad prudish. If you're not worrying about Rosalind seeing us, you're worrying about someone else."

Anne smiled, but the gibe about being a prude irritated her. She realized that open displays of affection were more acceptable now, but she was still operating on twenty-year-old dating rules. It was going to take some time to become used to these changes. Ben should understand that this was all new to her. Just because he could easily shift his feelings didn't mean she was able to. For a man who'd promised to be patient, he was certainly rushing her.

Ben carried the cake in one hand and clasped the other around Anne's waist as they went inside. Anne had to stop to take in the drama of his house. Even though it was a sharp contrast to her own traditional home, the architect within her was very impressed. Ben Weston had taken great care in the design of his own home.

The entry hall was a two-storied room with windows rising to the second level. The carpets and walls were a monochromatic cream color contrasted with green plants and showy flowers and with the shapes and textures of the furniture. On the walls were hung a number of paintings, mostly modern, all bold and colorful.

From the kitchen, glass-paned sliding doors opened onto a wooden deck, complete with a large gas grill. The aroma of mesquite and charcoal tantalized Anne's nose. She looked around the room and into the backyard. "Speaking of Rosalind, where is she?"

"Spending the night at Billie's."

"How come?"

"I wanted to be alone with you." He drew her into his arms. "We need some time to ourselves."

"Do we?" The prospect was unnerving. She had expected Rosalind to be there to serve as a buffer.

Anne had spent too much time over the past couple of days thinking, too much time reacting to what other people had said. She knew if she allowed Ben to kiss her, they'd wind up in bed, and her concerns would never be addressed. She could end up married to him all because of sex. And because he wanted a mother for Rosalind. To Anne, neither was sufficient reason for marriage. She pulled away. "Why don't you show me the house?"

"Should we start with the bedrooms?" His words were seductive, yet... Anne wasn't certain, but he seemed disturbed. The aloofness he cloaked himself with in the office seemed to settle about him.

"Whatever you like," she said, maintaining the same reserve.

The tour took half an hour, what with Ben's explaining why he'd chosen Mexican tiles for the bath or where he'd found the copper hood for the kitchen stove. It was easy to talk, architect to architect.

Ben started to relax again as he told her about his inspirations. Anne had often been impressed by the beauty of the restored building that housed Weston and Associates, but couldn't understand the lack of warmth Ben had brought to his own office. No photos, no mementos, just generic furnishings. His home was so different; it seemed to be Ben's personal statement. Obviously the real Bennett Weston lived here.

Fire and ice. That almost seemed to describe Ben. In the office or with acquaintances, Ben was always courteous, always professional, always...remote. But with those he cared about—Billie, Rosalind, Tyler, the Seguins, and now Anne—he was a completely different person. He'd told her about his upbringing, about his marriage, so it all made sense. He didn't trust easily, but when he did, he did so unconditionally.

By the time they returned to the foyer, he had his arm draped around her shoulder and was smiling. "Well, are you interested in moving in?"

"I must admit I'm impressed, but I'm still pretty fond of my own house," she answered.

"Did you live there with David?" He moved away from her and toward the bar.

"Yes. We bought the house from my folks. We'd just settled in before he left."

"Strawberry daiquiri?" As Anne nodded, Ben picked up the blender and added rum, ice and daiquiri mix.

Anne watched in silence as the blender whirled, then Ben poured the frosty pink mixture into stemmed goblets.

"You've never thought about remarriage?" he asked.

Anne was sitting on a bar stool, while Ben remained standing behind the bar. Both sipped their drinks slowly.

"No...not really. It would have been terribly wrong to consider something like that while David was still listed as missing. Then afterward, I had to adjust to being a widow. I guess I'm just beginning to get over it. Pretty slow of me, hmm?"

"Pretty loyal of you, I'd say. If he had come back, you'd have been able to hold your head high, standing by your man all that time. Nothing wrong with that."

Anne took another swallow of her drink. "What about you? You've been alone . . . how long?"

"Forever," he replied. "I was alone even when I was married. At least it seems that way. I was the one who brought Rosalind home from the hospital. Just Rosalind. Charlotte wanted no part of either of us. As soon as she could travel, she left town and never came back. Sounds like a soap opera, doesn't it?"

"Almost unbelievable." Anne shook her head slowly. "Especially the part about Charlotte abandoning her own child. I guess that really soured you on marriage."

"Oh, more than just marriage. I'm afraid that bitterness pretty much shadowed my relationships with women, period. I didn't realize how bitter I'd become until I met you. There was so much anger toward Charlotte. How could a woman be so cruel and manipulative as to use her unborn child to extort money?" He stroked his chin as if he were still unable to fathom the unthinkable.

"But I think I've finally put it behind me. Charlotte was just *one* woman. I have you to thank for showing me that." He finished his drink and set the glass on the counter, then circled the bar to where Anne was sitting. He pulled her from the chair and into his arms. "Marry me, Anne. Come live here with me. With us."

"Please don't . . ." She again eluded his embrace, this time crossing the room to stand by one of the large sofas flanking the fireplace. The discussion they'd had only emphasized what a short time they'd known each other, how much they still needed to learn.

"What's wrong?"

She didn't answer and he came to stand close beside her. "Don't you see, Anne, it would work."

"What makes you so certain?"

"Because you've made me trust again, because you've convinced me there are happy marriages, because we're good in bed together, because Rosalind needs you."

None of the reasons he listed made Anne feel any better. All she wanted was one reason—that he'd fallen hopelessly in love with her. Then she might be able to put her other concerns aside. But that was the one thing he didn't say. The only time he'd talked of love had been in the aftermath of passion. That hardly counted.

"And why should I marry you? So the boys would have a father, so I'd have a bed partner, so I'd have a man to take care of me?"

"You make it sound distasteful." He sat down on the couch and leaned back against the cushions, crossing his arms, a frown on his face. That defensive mien had returned, but Anne knew she couldn't let his forlorn look affect her decision. There was too much that needed addressing before she could agree to marry him. For now, they were at an impasse. Would Ben withdraw the proposal, she wondered, or just put it on hold?

Anne knew deep down that she didn't want him to change his mind. She wanted to marry him. She'd lost too many years of happiness with a man she loved to give up a second chance. *But David loved you back,* her conscience argued. *Ben doesn't.*

When Anne didn't respond to his statement, Ben continued, "Nothing to say?"

"I know it's trite, but this is all so sudden." She joined him on the sofa, settling in one corner and turning to face Ben. "One day you were acting like you wanted to throw me out of your office, then in little more than the blink of an eye, you were proposing to me!"

Ben took her hand. "That's not it at all. I was attracted to you from the start. *Too* attracted. I was disgusted with myself. I didn't want to be involved with any woman, particularly one I thought belonged to another man, other men. Anne, I'm ready for someone in my life. Maybe it seems like an about-face, but I've given this a lot of thought. In fact, I can't stop thinking about us being together."

"I need more time," she said.

"How much time? Another decade or two?" He stood up and towered over her. "You once accused me of being cowardly about involvement. That was pretty accurate and it forced me to think about my life, my values. But you, lady, should do some thinking, too. About letting go of the past.

"Every other word you speak is David. No wonder you won't consider marrying me—you're still married to him. For years you've nurtured some fairy-tale version of love, some fantasy marriage. Real life isn't like that."

"Maybe it could be," she answered. "I don't want to rush into anything, Ben. I don't want to make a mistake."

"We both know life holds no guarantees. Who knows what kind of marriage we would have? I'm willing to take a risk, to try to make you happy, but you, you're still in love with an illusion. That's the problem, isn't it?"

"Absolutely not! That's the most ridiculous thing I've ever heard!" She didn't like Ben's analyzing her. The problem between them wasn't her—it was Ben.

"I disagree," he countered, refusing to put the matter aside. "It takes a lot of living and a lot of reality to know if a marriage is a good one, Anne. Mine obviously wasn't, but yours was an unknown. If David had lived, you two might have been divorced by now; about half the couples in our age group are. He could already have replaced you with a younger wife. Some men do that, you know."

Anne jerked to her feet. "You're wrong! That never would have happened. David loved me intensely. How dare you try to get me to marry you by tearing down my relationship with him, by tearing *him* down. That's unfair and I won't let you get away with it. Why don't you admit that all you really want is a mother for your child and a warm body in your bed?"

"Is that what you think?" He went to the bar and poured another drink—straight bourbon this time.

She followed him, not quite understanding what had gone wrong. She *loved* Ben Weston. She knew she did. Why had she been so determined to argue with him, to push him away? "Ben, I'm sorry."

He responded stiffly. The warm caring Ben had disappeared. "Forget it. It's not the first mistake I've made. We might as well call it an evening. I'm not particularly in the mood to eat anymore, are you?''

"No," she answered, not knowing how to handle this withdrawal, but feeling a need to escape. Anne grabbed her purse and rushed out the door to her car, screeching the tires as she sped from the drive.

"YOU DROVE OUT HERE in this condition?" Tyler was already in his pajamas and silk robe, ready for bed when Anne pounded on his front door. "That road's dangerous when you're in total control, never mind when you're upset. You could have been killed!"

"Who cares?" Anne snapped, then broke into a sob.

"I do," Tyler soothed. "And so do the boys." He wrapped an arm around her and urged her inside the house and into the den. "Now sit down here and tell me what's wrong. Let me get you a brandy first, though. For medicinal purposes. You need something to calm you down."

By the time she'd finished the brandy, the tears had dried and Anne had once again regained her composure. "I'm sorry. I was acting like a silly schoolgirl."

"Well, I can't argue with that, but I guess in a way, I'm responsible." He sighed. "I try to throw two people I care about together—two people who need someone to love. Two people I think would be perfect for each other. Am I an old fool, or is it just that these people are both too pigheaded to admit they've found the right person?"

"Why? So Rosalind will have a mother, so James and Jody will have a father? Why?"

"Those would just be fringe benefits. Mainly so you and Ben will have someone to love."

"He doesn't love me."

"Oh? Did he say so?"

"No, he said he wanted me to marry him." Anne started crying again, but this time her sobs were interrupted by a fit of hiccups.

"He asked you to marry him, but he doesn't love you?"

"He only wants a mother for Rosalind. He'd do anything to make her happy."

"Even marry you? That's quite a sacrifice. But do you love him?"

"Of course I do! I'm the world's biggest idiot. I've fallen for someone who doesn't know what love is."

THE ATMOSPHERE at the office on Monday was chilly. Anne had come in early to place a letter of resignation on Ben's desk before he or anyone else arrived. She stayed in her office for the rest of the morning, but she could still hear Ben—first snapping at Mason, then roaring at poor little Lisa. By the time Anne left the office at noon for a long walk, everyone was treading warily, trying to keep out of the boss's way.

The December day was nippy, so Anne bundled up in a coat, scarf and leather gloves. The crisp air felt invigorating and she walked all the way to the state capitol grounds. As she turned back, Anne decided to circle around the Governor's Mansion, covering an additional mile before she returned to work.

Ben was waiting in her office when she arrived, standing by the window. Silently he watched her enter. Pretending to be unperturbed by his presence, Anne methodically took off her wraps and hung them on the coat tree, then sat down behind her desk.

"Your cheeks are red from the wind," he said softly.

She nodded in response. "Is there something I can do for you?"

Ben walked over to her desk. "I just wanted to ask you to reconsider your resignation. You've become a real asset to the firm. I don't think Carmen Seguin will be as excited about going ahead with the new house if you aren't here as her personal consultant." He smiled, though it looked forced to Anne. "If you'd like to take a break, maybe a couple of weeks off, to be home while the boys are here for the Christmas holidays, that will be fine."

"And you wouldn't mind?"

"Not as long as you agree to come back to work."

Anne paused. "Then I'd like to do that. Thank you." She didn't know why she suddenly felt so happy. Could it have something to do with Ben's not wanting her to quit? Did it mean there might still be a chance for the two of them?

"You're welcome," he said impassively. As he headed toward the door, his parting comment deflated her optimistic mood. "Why don't you start your sabbatical immediately? Things will be pretty slow until the first of the year."

"Okay, I'll start tomorrow," she said, her voice almost challenging.

This time Ben's only answer was a nod.

His conversation had been so stilted. And why did he tell her to "start immediately"? It sounded as though he wanted to be rid of her for a while. But what had she expected from him? Anne didn't know.

WITH EXTRA TIME on her hands, Anne threw herself into Christmas preparations. The twins would be home on Friday and she was determined to have the house completely decorated. Except for the Christmas tree. The boys always insisted on a huge one and she needed their muscle to get it into the house. Besides, they both loved Christmas so much, they'd be disappointed if there were no decorations to help with.

She worked from dawn to dusk, making sure she wouldn't have a minute to spare for uncomfortable or unhappy thoughts. She concentrated on decorating and shopping and cooking. Instead of just shuffling through recipes—divinity, fudge, date-nut candy, fingerprint cookies and bourbon balls—she actually began to make the calorie-laden goodies she tried to stay away from most of the year. She flitted from one project to another, yet she never got her mind off Ben. Or Rosalind.

Everywhere Anne went she noticed presents that would be perfect for the little girl. She found she couldn't resist picking up a few things—a doll, a child's book on whales, teddy-bear barrettes. She was uncertain about a gift for Ben. She doubted she should be concerned about it; she might not even see him over the holidays. Still, she didn't want to be embarrassed by receiving a gift from him and having nothing in return. But she just couldn't bring herself to choose something.

Maybe it was because she was trying her best to avoid even thinking about Ben. Every time she allowed him to enter her thoughts, she wanted to cry. She loved the man—really loved him. Maybe she shouldn't have been so reluctant to tell him that. Perhaps it would have made a difference. But he'd given up so easily that she was afraid to call him now. She wondered if he had changed his mind and decided he'd acted too hastily in proposing to her.

It was Thursday already and time for dinner with Tyler. This week they dined out. Tyler was at his most charming, obviously determined to cheer her up. Anne wondered if he could guess by the circles under her eyes how often she'd tossed and turned, a couple of times even crying herself to sleep. Surely the loose fit of her blouse was evidence of her recent five-pound weight loss. She tried to be lighthearted, filling him in on her shopping and other holiday preparations, inviting him to her place for a family party on Christmas Eve as well as the traditional Christmas dinner the following noon.

The evening was almost over before he finally asked about Ben. "Have you heard from him?"

She shook her head.

Tyler reached for her hand and held it a moment. "You will, honey. Besides, you can always call him—I can tell you miss the man. Maybe it's time for you to fish or cut bait."

Anne managed a wan smile. Tyler was so Texan, despite his English suits and Italian shoes and despite his self-made urbanity. The little idioms that slipped out from time to time were pure Southwest. Folksy or not, however, Anne knew that what Tyler had said came straight from his heart.

ANNE DIDN'T HEAR from Ben. The weekend came and her twins arrived home. "We're here, Mumsey. Ready to be waited on hand and foot."

Anne laughed. "Well, I hope you brought your own handmaidens with you. You're looking at a working woman, not a servant."

James turned to Jody. "Better get back in the car. No use staying if we're not going to be indulged."

"I'll show you indulged," Anne said, giggling. "Now come here, you two, and give your mother a big hug."

The three sat at the kitchen table, Anne with coffee and her sons wolfing down tuna-salad sandwiches and potato chips. Both asked about the Westons, but they didn't question Anne's evasiveness when she merely said she hadn't seen them lately. They didn't ask again. Within a couple of hours, they were out of the house and on their way to visit old high-school friends.

Their belongings were still in the hall where they'd dropped them. "Well," she said to Frank, "looks like I may be waiting on them, after all." She hoisted up a laundry bag and headed toward the utility room. But she was smiling and, for the first time in weeks, almost content.

Her parents arrived a few days later, and the cooking moved into high gear. Cheese straws, cinnamon buns, gingerbread men, homemade rolls, a conglom-

eration of holiday foods. Anne was already gaining
back the lost pounds, especially since her mother had
labeled her the official taster. It seemed as though
every time she opened her mouth, Faith Hargis was
sticking some sort of food into it. The house was full
and busy, the tree decorated, stacks of gaily wrapped
presents underneath. Pots of cheery red poinsettias
were placed throughout the rooms, the staircase railing was decorated with greenery, and bright twinkling
lights were strung outside.

Even the weather cooperated. Instead of the usual
mid-sixties, the temperature dropped into the thirties.
The windows were fogged with moisture, and Anne's
father kept a blaze going in the fireplace. It looked,
smelled, tasted like Christmas—but for Anne, it was
proving to be one of the loneliest in years. Having the
boys home, her parents visiting, two dogs, one cat and
five puppies underfoot didn't fill the gap. She missed
Ben. She missed Rosalind.

She'd visited the office one day, taking in a tray of
goodies she and her mother had made, and presents
for Billie and Lisa. But she came home more dejected
than ever. Ben wasn't there; he'd gone to El Paso.
Everyone teased her about her vacation and the
"special treatment" the boss had given her.

"We wish you'd hurry back, though," Hank said.
"We're not sure we can endure the old man much
longer. It's like he's in a permanent snit. What'd you
do to the guy, Annie?"

Although Hank had appeared to be kidding her,
Anne could tell he wasn't the only one interested in
what had happened between them. "Know what's

really bothering you all?'' she gibed. ''You guys just can't manage without the all-star rookie architect. Gotta go now. Merry Christmas!'' Even though she'd missed them, she felt relieved to escape.

TYLER WAS MAKING EGGNOG while Anne's mother spread the dining-room table with a buffet of meats, cheeses, fresh breads and vegetables. Bill, Anne's father, entered with a large silver chafing dish of tamales—a Christmas tradition borrowed from Texas Hispanics. He set the dish down and lit the fuel underneath, then immediately helped himself to the tamales.

''Bill Hargis,'' admonished Faith.

''I'm sorry, hon, I just can't wait.'' He removed the corn husk wrapper and bit into the masa-covered mixture of spiced meat. ''Heaven,'' he mumbled, his mouth full.

James and Jody had carried Tyler's stack of presents in from the car and were arranging them under the Christmas tree. Anne was the only one momentarily unoccupied when the doorbell rang, so she went to answer it. Her long red-and-green plaid taffeta skirt rustled as she moved across the room. She opened the door.

On the front porch stood Ben and Rosalind and Billie, holding a stack of presents. ''We thought we'd drop these off. We've just been to church,'' Ben said.

Anne smiled. ''Come in.''

As they entered the hall, Ben eyed the scene in the dining room. ''We don't want to disturb you. You have guests.''

"Just Tyler and my parents—from Arizona. Come meet them." She didn't want to lose Ben so quickly. Or lose Rosalind. The little girl was dressed in a white fun-fur coat. She had a pin with a Santa Claus face on her lapel and red ribbons in her hair. She looked adorable—like a little Christmas angel, Anne thought.

"Besides," she added, "I have some presents for you, too." She had finally bought a gift for Ben—an old architectural study of Austin, published seventy-five years ago. It wasn't an expensive present, but one she thought would please him.

They crossed under the mistletoe as they walked through the foyer. She noticed Ben looking up as they passed, but he didn't move to kiss her. She didn't know whether to be annoyed or relieved. She made the introductions and Tyler offered cups of eggnog. Her mother insisted the three of them stay and eat something; Ben looked at Anne for approval.

She agreed without hesitation. She wasn't ready for him to leave. He looked wonderful, dressed in a dark gray suit and red Christmas tie. Imagine, she thought, Bennett Weston in a gaudy red tie!

In spite of his festive attire, he did look a bit haggard, as though he, too, might have lost some sleep and some weight. The thought was not altogether unpleasant to Anne. She didn't relish the idea of suffering alone.

Rosalind and Billie followed Faith Hargis into the kitchen, Rosalind chattering happily. James and Jody were right behind them, James carrying a big red ribbon to wrap around Rosalind's puppy's neck. Debbie was one of the presents Anne wanted to give her. She'd been planning to send the twins over to the Westons on Christmas Day with the dog. Anne could hear Rosalind's squeals from the other room. "This is going to be the best Christmas ever!"

Tyler and her father were engrossed in building up the fire and debating the outcome of January's Super Bowl. This left Anne and Ben alone.

"Could we talk?" he asked.

She nodded, moving back into the hall with him. They stood by the steps of the stairway, leaning against the railing.

"I've missed you," he said.

"I've missed you, too."

"This time apart has damn near driven me crazy. I've been a bear at the office."

"So I've heard."

He ran his fingers along the sleeve of her red sweater. "Anne, I'm sorry for all those things I said. I had no right." He looked up and blue eyes locked with blue. "Can you just excuse them as the jealous grumblings of a man in love?"

"Are you saying you love me?"

His face showed surprise. "Well, of course I love you. What did you think my rushing you like that was all about? I'm crazy about you. I don't want to spend a minute away from you. I want you in my bed every night. Do you think you could love me a little, too?"

Anne smiled up at him. "Not a little, a lot. I love you, Ben. I've thought so much about what you said. I *have* been holding on to a dream. You offered me a second chance at love—at life—and I just didn't have enough sense to take it."

"It was more than that. I've done some thinking, too—I don't think I made myself clear enough before. I do want Rosalind to have a mother to love and to love her. I do want a family..."

"More children?"

"I'm happy with things the way they are, but if you want another child, that would make me happy, too. The only thing I can't face is a life without you, Anne. Will you be my wife? Will you stay with me, love me, for the next fifty years or so?"

"That sounds like just the kind of marriage I've always dreamed about."

Ben glanced at the family hovering around the dining table in the other room. "I want to kiss you—now."

"There's always the excuse of the mistletoe."

He looked up and sidled with her toward the red-trimmed berries, then took her into his arms. As his lips met hers, Anne knew her fears had been groundless. His kiss promised love and devotion, as well as the anticipation of a life together. The same promise of another kiss so many years ago.... Somehow Anne knew David would approve.

When the kiss broke off, Anne and Ben looked around to discover they had an audience. James and Jody, her parents, Tyler, Billie and Rosalind, holding her puppy, were watching them, all smiling.

Ben gave a mock growl. "Can't a man kiss a pretty lady under the mistletoe without drawing a crowd?"

"Sorry," Jody said with a chuckle, "we didn't realize we were interrupting a private holiday moment. Besides, the rest of us want to eat." Everyone laughed, and the whole group returned to the dining room, leaving the two of them alone once again.

Ben pulled Anne outside to the front porch. "Little did your sons realize what they were interrupting. Shall we go back in and tell them our news?"

Anne smiled. "Why not. Christmas is a season of love. Might as well share ours with everyone else." She put her arms around his neck and held her face up for another kiss. Neither seemed to mind the chill of the crisp air and the mist that had already brought a glistening film to the lawn. Anne only felt the warmth of Ben's embrace, the fire of his kiss.

After long moments, they separated. "I think Rosalind is right—this is going to be the best Christmas ever."

Anne had to agree as, arm in arm, they went back inside to their family.

HARLEQUIN Romance

This June, travel to Turkey with Harlequin Romance's

**THE JEWELS OF HELEN
by Jane Donnelly**

She was a spoiled brat who liked her own way.

Eight years ago Max Torba thought Anni was self-centered—
and that she didn't care if her demands made life impossible
for those who loved her.

Now, meeting again at Max's home in Turkey, it was clear he
still held the same opinion, no matter how hard she tried to
make a good impression. "You haven't changed much, have
you?" he said. "You still don't give a damn for the trouble you
cause."

But did Max's opinion really matter? After all, Anni had no
intention of adding herself to his admiring band of female
followers....

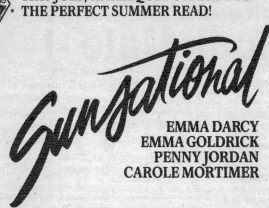